H_____ _____ _____ _____, ___ _____ _. "You damned right there's some bullsheet here, lady." He wanted to stop, jerk his hand out of the woman's hand and run back to the car. "What the hell am I doing at my age, running around in the middle of a bull pasture?" Pepe, Manuel and Tito skillfully lured the bull to the designated area by tossing stones at the bull, calling to him and when he hesitated, one of them ran past the bull's range of vision. The bull charged, nearly catching the man before he ran behind the tree trunk. The other men squatted, remained hidden, their capes ready to come to El Encanto's aid if he got in trouble. Chester peeked around the corner of the tree, almost into the bull's face, just as El Encanto called to the bull, opening up the fight season on a moonswept night, somewhere on the outskirts of Valencia.

Holloway House Originals
by Odie Hawkins

THE LIFE AND TIMES OF
CHESTER L. SIMMONS

ODIE HAWKINS

An Original Holloway House Edition
HOLLOWAY HOUSE PUBLISHING COMPANY
LOS ANGELES, CALIFORNIA

Dedication

To the Brothers,

> *Herbert Cross*
> *P.J. Robinson*
> *Ralph Vernon*
> *Fred Flowers*

and to the Sisters,

> *Lynn Flowers*
> *Yvonne Vernon*
> *D.A. Wesley*
> *Gladys "B.B." Lloyd*
> *Riva Akinshegun*

> *Real Friends*

Published by
HOLLOWAY HOUSE PUBLISHING COMPANY
8060 Melrose Avenue, Los Angeles, California 90046

International Standard Book Number 0-87067-341-6
Printed in the United States of America
Cover photograph by Jeffrey
Cover design by Bill Skurski

THE LIFE AND TIMES OF
CHESTER L. SIMMONS

Chapter 1

The hangover gong going off in his head was a reminder that Spanish wines were strong. He had decided to give himself a last night in Madrid, enjoying the city in a way that he could never have enjoyed it with Ife Ebuni. O well, I guess all is well that ends well. She's probably on her way to New York or Moscow by now and I'm on my way to Alicante.

He had made a spontaneous decision to go to Alicante because one of his writing idols, Chester Himes, had once lived there, wrote there and died there. If it was good enough for Chester Himes, its got to be good enough for Chester Simmons.

He ignored the hangover gong and opened his note book to read a couple of pages of subject titles he planned to deal with in Alicante.

"The Black Creative Personality"

"African based politics"

7

"Simone, A Love Story"
"The Art of Lying by an Expert"
"15 Years in the Joint"
"White Basic Bureaucracy"
"Velvet Dreams"
"Azania, Tomorrow's World"
"Black Flamenco"
"The Legacy of the Ancestors"
"The Survival Tango"
"Kujichagulia"
"Solid"
"I'm Hip"
"The Art of the Waiter"
"Crime and Too Much Punishment"
"The Survival Tango II"
"Bullshit!"
"The Writer Writes..."

He closed the notebook, unable to concentrate because of the rough motions of the bus and the hangover that was slowly going away. I'm going to write in Alicante, I'm going to seriously take a stab at something I've been threatening to do all of my adult life. He clenched his teeth together in a determined manner.

They arrived in Alicante at dawn. Alicante, a medium-sized city flush on the Mediterranean Sea, facing Algeria, the avenue that led to the cities of Moorish Spain: Muncia, Cartegena, Almeria, Malaga, Jerez de la Frontera, Cadiz, Huelva, Seville. He stepped from the bus station into the balmy warmth of the fall morning. Several cab drivers approached him but there was no swarming around, none of the New York City aggression.

"Taxi, Señor?"

"Do you speak Ingles?"

"Yes," the man answered with a sad smile, "Yes, I speak.

8

I learn in Texas.''

Chester carefully placed his three pieces of luggage in the trunk of the cab and turned to face-read the taxi drive as hard as possible. He looks honest and he looks old enough to know what the Real Deal is.

''What's your name, my friend?''

''Francisco Zurriaga, I am Basque.''

''You're what?''

''I am Basque, from the Pyrenees.'' He pantomimed the motions of someone playing the ancient Basque game called Jai Alai.

''The Pyrenees? You're a long way from home.''

''Yes.''

''How did you wind up in Texas?''

''Berry long story. Where do you wish to go?''

Chester had thought it out carefully; the best thing to do in a strange place is let it happen. ''Francisco, I don't really know where I want to go; comprende?''

''Yes, I understand.''

''But I can tell you what I need.''

The Basque tilted his beret down over his eyes, the sun was rising like an orange beam. ''Yes?''

''I need a decent, cheap place to stay, number one, and a good restaurant and maybe later...''

''Some womens?''

''Possibly.''

The taxi driver opened the door of his cab as though it were a Rolls Royce. ''Alicante, she is three parts,'' the driver drove along the beachside road, ''this is the beach where many womens come in the summer. They come from the north, Swedish, Danish, Aleman, Dutch womens. Big fun in the summer time.'' He made an abrupt left turn and suddenly they were in the heart of the city. ''This is El Centro, the heart.''

9

Chester stared at the pedestrians. They were obviously on their way to work but there was no frenzy happening, none of the U.S. madness to beat the clock. The driver pulled into a taxi zone, hopped out to open Chester's door.

"What's this?"

"I have not had my coffee." He laughed at the idea of pausing with his taxi driver to have a cup of coffee. Alicante was giving him good vibes. Inside the cafe Francisco exchanged grunted greetings with other drivers, the owner of the cafe. "You would like also un copita with your coffee?"

"Un copita? What's that?"

In answer, the driver signalled for two espressos and two cognacs ("dos copitas"). So this is the way you start your day off in Alicante.

"Now, I am saying to you about the place to live. The Residencia Norte is this way, three streets away. The price is not too much, not too little. I know, also another place in a home of a person. Very cheap. She is horrible women, but she is a good cook and her home, it is in the heart of the real Alicante."

"Good, take me there. How about another cognac?" He felt a strange sense of emotional attachment as the cab rumbled over the cobblestones into the old section of Alicante. Feels like I've been here before . . .

The taxi bumped to a stop in front of a building that looked like a medieval fortress.

"Pardon me, Señor, I must ask her to see you." A minute of paranoia settled on him. Am I being set up for something? Ten minutes later, the driver popped back out through the ancient doors of the fortress, followed by a woman who looked like an ancient Gypsy crone. Chester hopped out of the car to meet his new landlady.

"This is Señora Sanchez Bou-Gomez."

Chester bowed and gently shook the crone's hand. She looked to be about sixty-five in the face but her hands were young, maybe forty. And the twinkle in her eyes said twenty-five.

"She no speak much Ingles." They stood on the narrow sidewalk, staring from one face to the other. "Ask her how much she charges to rent a room?" The answer was the Spanish equivalent of $40.00 per week. Chester almost laughed aloud. After traveling with Ife Ebuni, her rent sounded like a tip. The deal was sealed with handshakes all around. Francisco wanted $10.00 Americano for his troubles and left Chester on the sidewalk with his luggage. "Señor, if you should wish a taxi, I am at the bus station or the Cafe Trabajero."

"I'll remember that, gracias, amigo."

He turned toward Señora Bou-Gomez as she picked up two of his bags and started walking up the steps of her apartment house.

"Wait! Just a minute! I'll get those."

"I am strong," she said in a graveled voice and kept going. The inside of the apartment building was like a half-finished dungeon, all the way up to the fifth floor, a shotgun apartment where the pigeons used to roost. She led him into the apartment without ceremony, stood beside him as he studied the dismal surroundings. It looked like thousands of ghetto apartments, except that this one was in Spain. What the hell, this is the real Alicante. She was renting him a bedroom and feeding him. He wasn't certain whether it was going to be breakfast, lunch and dinner or just one meal a day. From the looks of the surroundings he guessed it would be one meal a day.

After he had been allowed to take a complete look at the shabby apartment she led him through a short hallway to his bedroom. It wasn't bad. An Army cot, a table, a chair, a lamp, Black Forest print on the walls. She carefully placed his luggage at the foot of the cot and shuffled over to open the window. The window was covered by a wooden door that she braced open with a stick. She beckoned for him to come and look.

"Mira," she said, a glow on her ravaged features. At midday, he looked out onto the backyard of Alicante, into the heart of a Spain that hadn't changed for many, many years.

"Alicante," she said and left him standing there, looking at Gypsies prowling the alleys, men peddling things, people working, children playing simple games. Spain. He started unpacking. Maybe it won't be so bad after all. Once I get myself oriented, I ought to be able to trace Chester Himes' footsteps. Wonder how many people remember him? He paused to look out of his window several times as he unpacked. This was the first time he had had the opportunity to pause; to take the flavor of the place. There's got to be a whole lot to write about here. Moments later, feeling the urge to relieve himself, he strolled out of his room in search of the facilities.

Señora Sarafina Sanchez Bou-Gomez sat on the worn sofa, watching a Spanish soap, knitting a bit, chewing hard chocolate with the ten teeth she had on the top and the fifteen on the bottom. And drinking cheap wine.

"Uhh, pardonome, Señora, los caballeros, por favor?" She smiled at his rudimentary Spanish and pointed her glass toward the kitchen sink.

"Alli, there," she said. He looked from the sink back to her face and back to the sink. Am I really supposed to piss in the sink? She moved laboriously from the sofa to open a door off of the kitchen, to show him an outhouse. An outhouse instead of a back porch. He stepped inside the structure feeling very insecure. Damn, this motherfucker looks like something the birds built. She waited for him with a large pan of water near the kitchen sink.

"Pee pee or sheet?" she asked.

"Uhh, pee pee," he answered.

She poured the water into the sink and explained: "Pee pee, no flush, sheet, flush, comprende?"

"Sí, sí, yes, of course." The system worked simply. One used water from the kitchen sink to flush the toilet. Wonder what the deal is for toilet paper? I didn't see any in there.

The unpacking done, he sat in front of his "Alicante window" to scribble a few token lines in his notebook. *Arrived Oct. 3rd, rented an apartment (room) in the heart of the real Alicante, the landlady looks like a Gypsy crone.* He stopped writing, feeling slightly disoriented. What the hell am I doing here? You're here to write, that's why. Write about what? How in the hell should I know? The tape of the little voice in the back of his mind played out, leaving him with an unanswered question. He decided to take a walk, get a handle on the place he was in. Señora Bou-Gomez was exactly in the same spot he had last seen her, watching the soaps, drinking cheap wine. She signalled to him, to have a drink with her.

"Quieres vino, Señor?" His impulse was to refuse, but he had read somewhere that it was impolite not to share the native's hospitality.

"Uhh, sí, gracias, Señora, gracias." He watched her shuffle away to a cupboard for a glass. How old is this woman?

"Salud," she toasted him.

"Salud," he saluted her in return. Tilting his glass up for a drink of something that tasted like burgundy horse piss. Well, that's the last time for Tio Pepe. He waved off a second offering and started down the crumbling steps of the fortress. He hit the cobblestone streets a half hour before the beginning of Siesta, that two hour rest period in the middle of the day that most Spaniards consider sacred. The flavor of Tio Pepe gurgled up in his throat as he stumbled down the cobblestones to the beach. The taxi driver had given him a perfect description of Alicante. It was divided into three parts. He straightened his shoulders as he crossed the bridge to the beach.

God, no American wino ever drank anything as bad as Tio Pepe.

The beachfront walk was paved with a serpentine design. It wasn't Copacabana, it was Alicante. He walked slowly along the water's edge, mindful of the fact that he was directly opposite Algeria. Africa, home. The thought jarred him to a stop. Africa was the place he had told a thousand lies about, created people, places and situations that suited his fantasies. I have to get to Africa one day, he whispered to himself. The beachfront was a brief two mile stretch. He walked one way on the sand and walked back to his starting spot on the mosaic boardwalk, pausing for a cognac at both beachfront refreshment stands.

He had noticed an interesting phenomenon in Spain, in Europe. People drank all the time but there didn't seem to be any drunks. He sprawled on a bench, squinting into the sun, people watching. And watching the people watch him. The whole scene was interesting and he was really seeing it for himself for the first time. When he was traveling with Ife Ebun, life was swank hotels, restaurants, brief brushes against the common folks. He had to dismiss the experiences he had had with the Luxembourgers, the Belgians, the Dutch, Danish, Swedes, English, French and Italians, traveling with the diva. They were colored by his relationship to a famous person who happened to be Black. Now, for the first time, he was absorbing attitudes on a down-in-the-neighborhood level. The Spaniards didn't seem to be prejudiced, but he

14

knew enough about the history of the place to know that they were not completely innocent of bias. Everybody was biased, even if they weren't prejudiced. The difference here, he noticed, as well as in Denmark and Sweden, is that the bias was not completely racial. The northerners, the Danes and Swedes, English, French, loved color, he suspected, because there was so much grey in their foggy, winter blocked countries, which left people of color in a peculiarly favorable position. If they happened to be from America, for example, and they had money, they were eminently acceptable. However, if they were from Africa and poor, they were discriminated against, just as the Africans in America were. The Turks and Southern Italians in Germany and Sweden had found out how that worked, on a cultural level. The Africans in France had discovered it on the color level.

He sat there, his arms draped on the back of the bench, slightly buzzed on Tio Pepe and a couple cognacs, trying to steer his brain onto a great theme for a novel. Some people passed by and smiled at him. It was patronizing, he noted. It was rather like the smile of someone greeting a guest for dinner. Some people ignored him. They were habituated to seeing Africans sprawled on their beach front. A few of the women lingered near him, flashing wicked looks in his direction. He took it all in, noting the characteristics of each wave of glances. The pleasant types were granted a pleasant smile, the people who ignored him were patiently ignored in turn, and the women who lingered were offered promising smiles. He had nothing to lose. His novel was going to be about Spain and he wanted all of what Alicante was about to make it Spanish.

The city had dozed into Siesta as he made his way back up the cobblestones to his place in Alicante. He liked the place, it was lean, filled with age and tradition. He wandered around the city for a while, memorizing names, places, checking out the atmosphere. Finally he turned toward home, drowsy from Tio Pepe, the cognacs and walking in the sun.

Chapter 2

After three months, he felt like a citizen of Alicante. He had his favorite cafes, he could find his way around without asking for directions. He had developed a relationship with a loose woman who offered his sex drive somewhere to park every two weeks; he was beginning to speak a little Spanish and he had ground out four short stories. It seems that no one he spoke to had ever heard of Chester Himes.

He had designed a daily schedule that made him feel like a disciplined man of letters. Running on the beach before ten a.m., it was Mediterranean chilly now, in December, and often raining but never too fiercely to prevent him from running. A brisk toweling down after the run (there was no shower in the Bou-Gomez establishment, the kitchen sink solved all washing problems) and then a session of writing that lasted into the first hour of the Siesta. He shared the second hour with the rest of the town. Life seemed to be level, on an even keel, but he still felt vaguely uneasy.

17

"Why bullshit myself? I'll be fifty-one years old in July, no money in the bank, no investments, no insurance, nothing to fall back on." The insecurity was counterpointed by a kind of self-confidence that he could only credit to being in good health, physically and mentally. He would often sit in front of his Alicante window thinking about his life, the people he had known, the days and nights he had found himself in dark tunnels that seemed to offer no possibility of light at the end. And yet, he had found the light. "And I'm gonna find some light at the end of this tunnel, too."

Three weeks later, he had sold a short story about an African-American expatriate to a liberal left-wing English language newspaper being published in Madrid. He stared at the invoice, trying to magically transform 3,100 pesetas/twenty-five dollars, into $3,100 Americano. The first sale bolstered his nerve and pride one-hundred percent. I'm a writer. I've sold a story, I'm a full-fledged honest-to-goodness writer. It meant that he wouldn't have to hide his notepad when he went to El Canarios for dinner, he could scribble notes about the wildest ideas he could imagine and drink cognac, too.

"I'm a writer, I can do anything."

When the check came he gave himself a lavish, private $10.00 celebration. He decided not to go out with Ana, his loose woman, because she was beginning to create a little stickiness in their relationship.

"Cheester, you only come to me, wheen you want the pussie."

"I thought that's what you wanted, I mean, after all, lets face it, we can't get too involved. You have a husband in the Army, remember."

Alicante wasn't a great party hearty place. The people seemed to like the simple style. He had taken note of how Catholic and how regimented life was. Women and women's

18

things to do and men had men's things to do and they didn't switch around. He sipped his cognac. The Club Tropical was one of the few places that stayed open 'till two a.m., feeling grand and successful, at ease with his new found fame. He paused on the crumbling steps, stunned by the clarity of the idea. "I'm in Spain. I'll write about the bullfight." He brushed the thought aside momentarily. "No, that wouldn't be the right subject for me." He sat in front of his Alicante window, nursing a sherry nightcap. "Why not do the bullfight?"

The question followed him on his morning run, led him into the first hour of his writing day. What should my angle be? He became convinced that the subject would give him the big theme he needed. Now he needed to find a bullfighter or two. The bookstore gave him an unexpected bonanza of books on the bullfight and some valuable information came from the taxi driver, Francisco Zurriaga.

"Ahhh, Señor Cheester, the corrida is bery important to Spain, but only the Mexicans understand it also."

His interest became hypnotic, communal. His landlady, the Gypsy looking crone who consumed the horse piss called Tio Pepe was discovered to be a great aficionado and quite knowledgeable.

"With these eyes," she said in slow Spanish, "I saw Manolete and Carlos Arruza, mano a mano." He was forced to share many glasses of Tio Pepe, listening to Señora Bou-Gomez tell him what the art of bullfighting was like in the good ol' days. "In those days, my friend, the bulls were as large as cathedrals and the men had cojones. Sabes?" He nodded as often as necessary to let her know that he did understand what she was talking about and dutifully sipped his piss. "In those days, the aficion was honest, inteligente. Sabes?"

"Sí, yes, yes."

19

"The corrida was respected and the men who fought the bulls were almost like priests, especially the Gypsies."

"Why the Gypsies?"

She poured herself more Pepe and used the moment like a great actress.

"Because. The Gypsies in Spain, like the Africanos in America, have more alma."

"Alma? Soul?"

"Sí, alma, soul."

One evening, under the influence of one Tio Pepe too many, she stood in the center of the narrow living room floor and using her manta, showed him the difference between the capote and the muleta. "Antonio Ordonez and the Mexicans, Manuel Capetillo and Luis Procuna were great muletaros." She displayed elegance as she made a silky veronica. Suddenly, the years of wine gluttony and overeating disappeared as she sucked her stomach in and leaned into a thousand pound Miura with her right foot. "That was the way Manolete did it. They say this pass was named for the woman who wiped the sweat from our Lord's brow as he was going to be crucified. You see how the capote leads the bull, almost touching his horns as he charges."

He could see it, he could see the interweaving of the religious feeling, the masculine principle that the bull represented, the monster that the crowd was, the depth of the emotions that the sight of blood provoked. He grew a beard and discovered that the print in the books was becoming blurred, he needed glasses. He decided to go for the Ife Ebun-Ben Franklin specs.

Ana, the loose woman, released his romantic obligation to her with a half-hour of vicious behavior. "I knew you were not the one for me from the beginnings. You men are all alike, no matter, Black, Spanish, Yellow or whatever!"

"But Ana, what about your husband?"

She ignored the question and pushed him out of the door. "And I neber want to see you again! Neberrr!"

It was all falling into place, neatly and smoothly. He was reduced to visiting one of the city's respected whorehouses periodically, but he felt the savings of emotional time was worth the impersonal treatment of his sexual urge.

He had decided on his method of approach, he wanted to approach the subject from the inside. It was impossible for him to consider the idea of becoming a bullfighter, the next best thing for him to do was attach himself to a bullfighter. But where to find one? The bullfighters lived in the bullfight kingdoms, Madrid, Seville, Cordoba.

"Francisco, you know any bullfighters?"

The taxi driver pulled his beret down over his eyes and worried the question through his Basque mind for a minute. "Sí, I do know a bullfighter."

Chester excited, pressed the taciturn taxi driver who had learned his English in Texas. "You do?! What's his name? Where is he?"

"Well, I must be above the board, you know."

"Yes, of course, above board, I understand."

"This one I know, he ride in my taxi twice. His name is Ernesto Suares, El Encanto, and sometimes he is bery good and sometimes, you know, no so good."

"He sounds like the perfect one, where can I find him?"

"He retired at the ends of last season."

"He retired?"

"Yes, but he will not be retired so long, he loves to fight."

"Then why did he retire?"

Zurriaga made a characteristic Alicante pause. He was beginning to discover the pause was not an affectation, it was simply the pace of their lives.

"He was afraid." Chester waited for a few beats, to allow the rest of the sentence to surface.

21

"You say he was afraid?"

"Sí, he was afraid."

Once again he allowed the pause ample space before cutting back in. "He was afraid of the bull, naturally."

"Sí, we are all afraid of the bulls naturally and only a few can overcome this fear."

"I understand that, but why would a man fight bulls if he is afraid?"

Francisco shrugged. "Hunger is a powerful way to kill fear."

"But you say your man was afraid. Did his hunger overcome his fear."

"No, Señor, no hunger could overcome El Encanto's fear. He was the master of fear."

"You mean he was afraid and no one was more afraid that he was."

"Exactly. He was the master of fear."

Chester sipped his cognac, trying to figure out a way to break through the semantical barrier. "Francisco, let me ask you a question. If the man you are speaking about is so afraid of the bulls that he had to retire, how can you consider him a good bullfighter?"

"I say he is bery good because sometime, maybe one fight in one-hundred fights, he will conquer his fear and create a faena that is incredible."

"And that one fight makes him great?"

"Sí."

"I don't understand, I'm missing something."

Francisco Zurriaga, the Basque from the Pyrenees, adjusted his beret and spoke slowly, in Spanish and then translated himself into English. "For a man to fight bulls who is not afraid is nothing. The faena lacks emotion, but when a man is afraid and is willing to fight despite that fear, that is something. That is what El Encanto can do, sometimes.''

"Where does Ernesto Suares, El Encanto live?"

"He lives in Valencia.''

Chester spent a full week, sipping Tio Pepe with his landlady, listening to stories about Ernesto Suares, El Encanto, preparing a point of attack for the novel to be.

"Ahh, El Encanto,'' she spat the name out between the spaces where her teeth had been. "El Encanto is a coward. He has always been a coward. And he will always be a coward.''

"But I've heard a few people say that he has given a few fights in his life that were the talk of the taurine world?''

A weird light shot into her eyes. "Yes, this is true. I saw one of them. It was in Seville and on that day he would have given the bath to Joselito, Manolete, Gaona, any of them.''

Chester felt disoriented. Maybe it's this rotten horse piss she's got me drinking. How in the hell could a man be the worst in the world and the best at the same time?

"The bulls were Miuras, you know the breed? They are said to be man killers.'' He snatched up one of his bullfight books to show her a picture of the breed she was talking about. "Yes, the Miuras, very powerful, very intelligent, very dangerous. Some people say they know Latin, they are so smart.'' They shared a laugh as she refilled their glasses. Better be careful with this stuff, I might begin to like it. "El Encanto was fighting mano a maño against Manolo Giron, one of the best and bravest fighters from the family of fighters. His father was a matador, his grandfather was a matador, his great-grandfather had been a matador and two of his brothers were matadors. As you can see, the bulls were in his blood.'' The eerie sound of the Gypsies singing, who lived three houses away, gave the Señor Bou-Gomez story a special auditory effect. "In the mano a mano, as you know from reading your books, each matador fights three bulls

23

alternating. Giron was wonderful with his first bull, he placed his on sticks and gave a beautiful demonstration of how to play a powerful, hard-charging bull. El Encanto, with his bull, did nothing. Nada.

"He didn't put his own banderillos in and when he tried to perform fancy passes with the muleta, his feet moved like a tap dancer. It was almost the same with the next two bulls. Giron could do not wrong and El Encanto could do nothing right."

Chester took careful note of how sarcastically she pronounced El Encanto, the enchanted one.

"At one point, El Encanto actually dropped the muleta to the ground and ran away from the bull."

"You mean he actually ran away?"

"Let us say he made many steps backwards." The gravelly voice of the storyteller laughing gave him Twilight Zone chills. "The aficion, the fans, screamed curses at his cowardice and threw things at him. They were angry because he was betraying the whole idea of the corrida. The aficion, the people come to see a man do what they are unwilling, or are afraid to try to do. And El Encanto betrayed that idea. I cannot tell you how many times he stabbed the bull with his sword before the bull finally collapsed. I did notice a strange thing, however. My father always used to buy the best seats and from where we were sitting I could see tears rolling down El Encanto's cheeks.

"Obviously, he took pride in what he had chosen to be. For the third bull for each of them, there were bulls from the old days, real animals. Giron did all that was possible for him to do with his bull. He gave us faroles and pases de muerte and the trick pass that Manolete had made popular, the looking-at-the-crowd pass. Giron made it his own by looking down at the bull as he passed and then looking at the crowd. And then looking back at the bull *en redondo*.

"The word, even in Spanish, sounded different, interesting, to go around and around en redondo.

"We screamed, not believing that he could do such work, no one could. He was cold and precise and we loved everything he did. We even loved the way he killed. It was precise, almost surgical." The aficion granted him an ear and the tail. The Madrid aficion was knowledgeable and complex. An ear and a tail was an expression of high regard.

"El Encanto, to cope with Manolo Giron's triumph, met Julieta on his knees. As the bull charged into the arena, El Encanto sprawled on the ground in front of the gate that the bull was being let out of, capote in his hand, dead drunk. For those of us who realized the state he was in, there was a feeling of shame. After all, we were Spaniards and there was no need to be drunk to do our national art. Bullfighting is to Spain, you understand, my friend, as what Capoeira is to Brazil."

Chester wobbled back to his seat, Tio Pepe spinning in his head, happy. So, this is what comes out of the crone's pad. He had put up with badly cooked food (though Francisco said she was a good cook, maybe that's their bake-off together, I wonder if they're fucking. Naww, not "Fina," she only fucked once in her life and that was too heavy, too bad, she might've had some good pussy in the long ago, too bad.)

"He stumbled to his feet. I can see it as though it were yesterday. And planted himself as though he were a tree and performed six pases de la muerta, alternating from left to right, that caused six people in the audience to have a heart attack. My father was one of them. They took him out but he told us, "stay with this, El Encanto is becoming a miracle today."

Chester excused himself to use the facilities. He'd never been aware 'til he arrived in Alicante, Spain, how interesting his dick was. In Spain, living with a sixty some year old widow, there was a strong suspicion that he was jewwgging the widow. He wasn't, and thought, as he held his stuff out to piss, she ain't my type. But her stories were on the money. "El Encanto became a mythical figure that afternoon. He demonstrated for the poor and homeless, he made pleas for funds for the aged, those with AIDS, Africans, Asians, Europeans, everybody. He said, 'Join my world and feel how close death is to you.' He made the bull pass so close to him that there were moments when it seemed that the bull had become one. He was part of the bull's horns, he was the bull's brother. They had developed an unknown dance between a bull and a man. The crowd screamed with each pass, afraid to feel the emotion of a horn puncturing their guts.

"El Encanto ignored their demands/urges and placed more complicated ideas in his mind. He had always wanted to fight a bull blind.

"He paused in the middle of his faena, the bull still strong after one pic and two well placed banderillas, and strutted to the barrera, his muleta at half mast.

"'Gitano! Tie your handkerchief over my eyes!' Gitano, the Gypsy swordhandler stared at his matador for a second and then whipped his handkerchief out and tied it around the matador's eyes. Everyone in the arena was screaming, No! No! No! Don't do it! Don't do it! But it was too late, he was doing it.

"He used the muleta as though it were a radar and with wrists of steel, he played the bull back and forth, his snout following the muleta as though it was a garden gate and he was being let in."

Chester held his glass at half mast, trying to decide if she were putting him on, or what. Blindfolded, fighting one of the most dangerous animals in the world? "You say he had himself blindfolded?"

26

"Yes, he did. I saw this. And with the blindfold on, he performed the most complicated, dangerous passes, the Arrucina, naturales en redondo, the Manoletina, a farolades with the left and right hand. We screamed ourselves hoarse. And when he felt we could take no more, he pulled the handkerchief from his eyes and used it as a lure to kill the bull with one perfect thrust."

She had helped him make a decision. "Yes, I'll write about the bullfight and Ernesto Suares will be my model." He explained his plan to Señora Bou-Gomez.

"Hah! You will be lucky to find him sober, if you can find him at all."

Valencia was only two-hundred miles to the northeast, he was going by bus and he was going to find El Encanto, become his friend, do his story.

"Francisco, where would I find Ernesto Suares?"

The taxi driver who had become his advisor, cultural historian and Spanish guide, pondered the question, offered his Alicante Pause. "I would say to you, my friend, there are two places you may find Ernesto Suares. In a bullfight bar or between some womens' legs."

Chester paid his landlady three months rent and tripped off to Valencia on the bus. He stared out at the vineyards, rolled his eyes to heaven and at the sight of the modern towns, the Benidorms and Denidorms. Disgusting shit.

He liked Spain, he felt at ease there. The people were warm, not excessively friendly and life was spare, lean, orderly. There was no false effervescence going around, no back slapping, and fake embracing. Strange, he thought, that racism was not an issue in Spanish life. It was there, but it was directed at the Gypsies. In Alicante, across the sea from Africa, on the southeast coast Spaniards were quite used to seeing dark faces. A lot of their faces had been darkened by eight-hundred years of African influence. And they hadn't

27

left a residue of ill will about their colonization. The Gypsies, who seemed to have continued something the Moors started, artistically, were scapegoats. He found the anti-Gypsy bias a little hard to deal with. Spain loved her music, loved her philosophical statements about life, but didn't like the Gypsies.

He decided on the bus to Valencia, to do a book on the subject, someday. Valencia struck him as being a larger Alicante. It was obviously a more important city than Alicante, but he could automatically tell the difference between the natives and the visitors. His cab driver could have been Francisco Zurriaga's brother, and when he asked, "Where can I rent a room, cheap, in the real Valencia?", the man didn't hesitate to take him to a seedy hotel in the heart of one of Valencia's oldest barrios. It was a neighborhood where people hung their washing from balcony to balcony, women gossiped from door to door, children ran ragged in the street and the men spent some part of every day at the local bodega.

The Hotel Valencia treated him as though he were visiting royalty and the treatment got better after he claimed a third floor room for two months. He even worked out a deal to have his sheets changed every other day. The next day he set out to walk around the city. The weather was brisk and traffic moved more rapidly than the traffic in Alicante. He spent the day strolling up and down avenues, pausing in cafes for cognac and espresso and when the mood hit him, asking, "Where do the bullfighters go to drink?"

"I'm sorry, I don't know where the bullfighters go, would you like another cognac."

He returned to his room at twilight with a whole broasted chicken (a la Valenciana), a bottle of good red wine and *La Opinion Valenciana*. After half the chicken and two glasses of Rio Negro, he sat in the window, his arms folded on the window sill, like an old woman, watching Valencia go about its post-siesta business. The city was lively, no doubt about that; the women were fashionable and beautiful and the men were macho but didn't seem to be chauvinistic to a fault.

It was Friday evening and like all poor neighborhoods all over the world, music was bursting from the seams. Michael Jackson, or a facsimile, was thrilling groups of teenagers clustered around an obviously popular shop. He couldn't tell what it was from his angle. A type of Spanish music with lots of accordions in it was coming from another angle and from down the hall, the yearning sounds of some serious flamenco. He poured himself a third glass of Rio Negro and turned it.

Life is a motherfucker. Nobody, not even my momma, could've told me that I'd be sitting up in a hotel room in Valencia this evening, digging Spain from the third floor. Titles for poems, novels, short stories, articles, plays, essays, love letters, flashed through his head, coupled with chapters that no one had written yet, nor were they likely to write. Ideas flickered through his brain, triggered by the rich red burgundy. Long, slow thoughts clashed with arrangements he wanted someone else to make. He felt gloriously high.

The night life in his neighborhood intrigued him. He could keep his eyes on the entrance to the Club Niño and be certain that he would witness some kind of disturbance every half hour. The latest scene involved a regulation brawl. It seemed to be about one woman discovering that her man was about to enter the club with another woman. He laughed aloud, drinking his fifth glass of wine. "Shit! This is Spanish Harlem, f'real!"

The next day an attack of logic, overshadowed by a slight burgundy hangover, caused him to take a taxi to the Valencia bullring, hang around for a bit (it was Monday and nothing happening) and find out where the bullfight crowd was.

"The matadors and their cuadrillas? You must go to the Cafe Gallo."

He made a low-keyed entrance at the Cafe Gallo later that evening, carefully checking out the clientele as he draped his elbows over the fifty yard long bar. This was obviously one of the full-fledged taurine joints. The wall behind the bar was lined with the stuffed heads of bulls and pictures of fighters, ancient and now, fighting bulls. He sipped a cognac and nodded pleasantly to the eyes that met his eyes. One of the things he'd found out early on was not to be closed in, introverted, if you wanted something from people. The Cafe Gallo was a man's place and all of the women (fourteen out of a total of seventy-five patrons) were obviously whores or women who were imitating whores. The place was musty with cigar smoke and sherry, funky in the Black jazz man's sense of the word. Men with scars on their cheeks, working men's caps cocked over their ears or berets, drank cognac neat or sherry. A guitarist strummed listlessly in a distant corner.

One of the women caught his eye and flirted for a moment. He turned away from her seductive look to stare at a beady-eyed bull that had a pair of horns that looked like antlers. The last thing I need up in here is a "situation" about some woman's playful mood. Several of the men seated at nearby tables caught the exchange, or lack of it and nodded their approval. Women were obviously born to be tempting but there was no need to surrender to their appeals. They exchanged cold smiles with him when their eyes crossed again. The Spanish male knew the power of women, and what they were put here for, or so many of them thought.

After an hour of cognacs, small talk with the bartender (Yes, I am an American, I'm an African-American) and a trip to the men's room, he decided it was time to make his move.

"Bartender, what time does Ernesto come in?"

"Señor, many Ernestos come to Cafe Gallo."

"I'm talking about Ernesto Suares."

The bartender wrinkled his nose in disgust. "Ah, that one! Sometimes he comes early, sometimes late."

Chester suddenly felt elated, he was in the right place at the wrong time. "Thank you," he said, and wobbled out, buzzed on eight cognacs. But in the right place.

Three evenings later, at 11:15 in the night, Ernesto Suares, El Encanto stumbled into the Cafe Gallo, a fat cigar in the corner of his mouth, a bit tipsy, the woman who had flirted with Chester on his right arm. Chester, a little high himself, followed the direction of the bartenders pointing chin. That is Ernesto Suares. He made a surreptitious study of El Encanto as he occupied a table, signalled for drinks and continued an animated conversation with his companion. Chester was surprised to discover that El Encanto was a young man, he couldn't be older than thirty-five, that he was matinee-idol handsome and that the people around him seemed to like him. He must've gotten into the ring when he was a baby.

The atmosphere of the Cafe Gallo seemed to warm up with Suares' presence. He made loud jokes, flirted with other women behind his lady's back, tilted his head back for glass after glass of cognac. And in between times, he argued about the merits of other, older bullfighters. Chester felt at ease with the language, the atmosphere. He still had trouble saying everything he wanted to say, but he had no difficulty understanding what was being said.

"Yes, of course, Don Miguel was an assassin with the steel, think about all of the practice he had had with those American college girls." The rhythm of the language tipped him to where the punch lines were. He was enjoying himself from a distance. Once, twice, Suares made a point of catching his eye. The third time, he flashed Chester a dazzling smile and held his cognac glass up for an across-the-cafe toast. Chester returned the gesture.

This one of them charmin' motherfuckers, totally charmin'. He had known a few charmin' motherfuckers in the joint. They were the kind of people who could get away with almost anything because they were charmin'. No one had ever been able to put a label on the origin of the quality, some had it, most didn't. The Cafe Gallo was beginning to fill up, the talk was becoming cruder and louder and the guitarist seemed to have opened up on a vein of serious flamenco. Chester scanned his head for a way to approach El Encanto. I can't just go over and start rapping, he would take me to be just another tourist chump. The bartender solved the problem. "Would you care for another cognac, Señor?"

"Yes, I would like another one, and I would like to have a bottle of your best cognac taken to Ernesto Suares' table." The bartender's eloquent shrug and the expression that flickered across his face said one thing, "You're stupid." The bartender took the bottle of Soberano over to Suares' table and made an elaborate presentation. Suares immediately opened the bottle, poured drinks for the trio who had joined him and weaved over to Chester, a glass of cognac in each hand. He handed him the glass with immense dignity and then offered a toast.

"I hope that there should always be some of this blood to warm our blood."

"I hope so, also," Chester replied as they poured the cognacs down.

El Canto smacked his lips together, relishing the after taste of the cognac. "Only a few people in the world really appreciate good cognac."

"I agree."

32

The guitarist slammed into a few chords that sounded like Muddy Waters at his best. Ernesto Suares ran a shrewd eye across Chester's face, checked his clothes out. "You're Americano, no?" he asked in a thick Andulusian accent. Chester, surprised to hear him speak English, nodded quickly.

"Yes, yes, I am an American. I didn't know you spoke English?"

"More or less. I also speak some French and Italian. In Europe, one must be be...how you say? Verse-till?"

"Versatile."

"Yes, exactly."

Ernesto's friends shouted across the cafe for him to rejoin them. Suares made a neat little Asian bow. "My friends want me to come back. Thank you for the cognac."

"You're welcome."

He took three steps away from Chester and then slowly turned as though he were leading a bull past his body. "Perhaps you would like to join us, my friend. What is your name?" Chester eased off the barstool.

"My name is Chester Louis Simmons and I already know that you are the great El Encanto."

"So, the fame of El Encanto has traveled to America also."

"And beyond."

They strolled across the cafe, talking as though they had known each other for years, their tongues oiled by an uncounted number of cognacs. Well, the first part is solved, he knows me and I know him. Let's see where it goes from here. Suares introduced him as though he were an old friend. The flirtatious woman's name was Carmen Albacin and she lived up to her reputation while they were being introduced. These were not freeloaders. They were not Ernesto Suares' dearest European friends, in the Ife Ebuni sense of that

33

tradition. These were old friends, people who had withstood the pain of remaining close during his worst moments. They left the Cafe Gallo after the bottle of cognac was finished, wandered into another bar for another bottle of cognac. Chester was high but feeling competent. They pub-crawled through the night and wound up in a twenty-four hour restaurant that was Spain's version of Denny's. They were bleary-eyed, clumsy from alcohol and famished. The entourage had withered down to a trio, Carmen Albacin, El Encanto and Chester.

"Well, my friend," Ernesto Suares said to him in English, "we are at the time of food and women, but first, food." He was beginning to feel the need for a long, deep sleep, but a cup of coffee and the urge to see the situation through to the end prevented him from packing it in. He was fascinated by El Encanto's capacity for gusto. The man literally seemed to have no bottom. He had decided not to reveal himself, to explain that he wanted to write about the life of a bullfighter, about the corrida. The moment of truth was ahead.

El Encanto let out a low-keyed belch after a breakfast of soup and bread, and turned to Chester with a gleam in his eyes. "Now then, we have satisfied our appetites, it is time to satisfy our desires."

Is he serious? Yes, he is serious. Chester paid the check, a habit he had picked up during the course of the night, and followed El Encanto and Carmen Albacin out onto a dawn-streaked street. Now what?

"Well, are close enough to your place to walk?"

Chester involuntarily blinked with surprise. "My place? I don't understand."

Ernesto Suares pulled him off to one side, leaving the lady to freshen her make-up in a shop window. He whispered urgently, "We need a place to take this woman. I have no place." Chester didn't know whether to laugh out loud or frown silently. So this is what hanging out with the great El Encanto is all about.

"Okay, we can go to my place, but I have no idea where we are right now."

"Tell me your address."

The bullfighter and the lady looked at him. It was their turn to be surprised. "The Hotel Valencia? That is in the heart of the old section."

"That's where I live, on the third floor."

"We'll have to take a taxi."

Chester felt alternately pissed and proud as they were driven through the early morning streets, El Encanto and the lady asleep in the rear of the taxi. Well, I got what I wanted and I'm paying for it. He suspected a little game was being run on him, but the cost at this point, was so small that he felt he'd be able to deal with it.

"Belly up, my friends, belly up! We're here!" He paid the fare and led the pair, all three of them sleepy and half drunk, up to his room. The woman, her eyes fuzzy, took one look at the bed and did a careful striptease, placing her clothes neatly across the nearby chair. Ernesto Suares, trying to look lascivious, stepped out of his clothes, leaving a pile in the middle of the floor.

Chester felt his flesh crawl, looking at El Encanto's body in soiled cotton briefs, at the scarred welts on the inside of his thighs, across his chest and stomach. One long wound looked as though it had been sewn by a Dr. Frankenstein. He wanted to ask him about the scars, talk about the esoterica of the bullfight, but there was no time. El Encanto had snuggled under the blankets next to Carmen Albacin and they were both snoring like woodcutters. Chester stood at the foot of the bed, creating titles for his novel-to-be . . .

"The bullfighter and the Lady/Whore"

"Nights in the Saloons of Valencia"
"El Encanto's Magic"
"The Bulls of the Dawn"

He surrendered to fatigue at "Warriors of the Bottle" and settled into bed on the opposite side of Carmen Albacin, who cuddled him into her funky left armpit as though she were a motherbird and he and El Encanto were nestlings.

Chapter 3

Chester's room became El Encanto's convenience station for a few days. It seemed to have developed so artlessly that he couldn't believe that El Encanto had planned it.

"Chester, please don't misunderstand. There are places I could go, including home to my wife, but I cannot go at this time." And, as suddenly as he had asked to spend a few nights, he was gone. Chester was severely pissed.

"Damn! You mean to tell me that I've spent good Spanish money on this jive ass motherfucker and he disappears." They had edged up on the subject of a book on the feelings of a bullfighter once or twice, during marathon cognac drinking sessions, but El Encanto slid away from it by gently announcing, "No man can put into words the fear a man has in front of a bull." And now he was gone, strayed back to his old set. Chester wandered about the city for a couple days, going to movies, sitting up in cafes, drinking cognac and espresso and trying to put another angle together.

No, it's got to be El Encanto's story. What does a proven coward do in the bullring? Here is the story in three hundred pages or less. He made his way back over to Cafe Gallo. The bartender gave him that wise guy look, "See there, fathead, I could've told you you were going to be given the bath." But there was other news...

"Ernesto Suares has gone back into training. He is no longer retired. He will be fighting bulls from the Domeco finca in the spring."

Chester felt strangely exhilarated. Now how do I get back in touch with this crazy son-of-a-bitch? The solution occurred as spontaneously as the question. El Encanto made his usual appearance that evening, a different woman in hand, grinning.

"Ahh, Chester, my friend, it is so good to see you. I have missed you. Where have you been?"

Chester decided not to remind Ernesto that he had not been the deserter. He decided to get some information first. "I've been around. I hear that you're back in training, that you've come out of retirement. Is it true?"

Ernesto made a comically sad face and shrugged. "Yes, I have returned again, for the last time."

"Where are you training?"

El Encanto made a mischievous face and snapped a devilish wink at Chester. "Where am I in training? Well, tonight I'm starting here." Chester matched the raucous laugh that El Encanto released. This is the one I'm going to write about. I'd better keep my eye on this guy.

Chapter 4

During the course of the following days and nights, Chester made himself a part of El Encanto's lifestyle and suffered.

"Damn! Where does this dude sleep?"

One night, after a bottle of cognac, El Encanto announced, "Now is the time to go to the bulls." Chester followed the quintet (Ernesto, his latest "Carmen" and three men who were members of this cuadrilla) out to a car and before long they were on the outskirts of the city.

"Ernesto, where are we going?"

"To the bulls," he answered without hesitation.

Chester decided to relax and absorb, rather than worry and speculate. There was no telling what would happen with El Encanto. They rode through the Spanish countryside, nursing the cognac bottle that someone had thoughtfully brought along. They sang songs about hard-hearted women, the joys of wine and the bulls and the inevitable approach of death. On the moon-blanched road in the middle of nowhere, the driver rolled to a slow stop. "We are here," El Encanto whispered to him. "We are here."

Chester looked around for a house, a place where people lived. There was only moonlight and open pasture.

"We are here?" Chester whispered back.

"At the bulls," he answered. The woman giggled at Chester's ignorance. Chester shook his head and shrugged. Here we are, out in the middle of nowhere and he's talking about bulls. The thought struck him—we're on a bull ranch, a finca. It was the sort of thing he had read about in the bullfight novels. The espontaneo who goes into the pastures at midnight to secretly hone his skills. The matador and his men retrieved their capotes from the trunk of the car. Ernesto Suares made an impulsive decision to use the muleta, the half-sized cape, rather than the larger capote. "I want to feel my wrists work more."

The six of them hiked through the open field under a moonshine that was so bright he felt as though he was in a different kind of daylight. "There, there is one," the woman at his side whispered. Everyone paused to stare at the animal glowing in the moonlight, about seventy-five yards to their right front. Ernesto Suares took charge, the general giving orders to his troops.

"Manuel, Pepe, Tito, bring him to that flat surface area near the olive tree."

"Which olive tree, matador?" one of the men asked, his voice shaking a bit.

"That one, to the left of the flat surface. What's wrong, Pepe, are you blind?"

Suddenly, Chester became aware that they were in the middle of a pasture with a wild animal who was faster than a race horse over a short distance, weighed fifteen-hundred pounds or more, bone dry, had horns that could pierce metal and was extremely ill-tempered when disturbed. He felt

40

small, vulnerable, scared shitless.

El Encanto's men fanned out to approach the bull, to line it the designated area. "Blanca, Chester, I want you two to go to that tree, you will be safe there." He spoke in Spanish and English. Blanca, a veteran of these impulsive excursions, grabbed Chester's hand and pulled him along. He clutched the cognac bottle, three-fourth's empty, in his other hand. "If this motherfucker charges, I'm gon' hit him in the head with this bottle, so help me God!" Blanca seemed to be enjoying the experience.

"Careful here! There are some bullsheet."

He felt the urge to laugh, but couldn't. "You damned right there's some bullsheet here, lady." He wanted to stop, jerk his hand out of the woman's hand and run back to the car. "What the hell am I doing at my age, running around in the middle of a bull pasture?" Pepe, Manuel and Tito skillfully lured the bull to the designated area by tossing stones at the bull, calling to him and when he hesitated, one of them ran past the bull's range of vision. The bull charged, nearly catching the man before he ran behind the tree trunk. The other men squatted, remained hidden, their capes ready to come to El Encanto's aid if he got in trouble. Chester peeked around the corner of the tree, almost into the bull's face, just as El Encanto called to the bull, opening up the fight season on a moonswept night, somewhere on the outskirts of Valencia.

"Eh Hayyy toro! Eh hayyy!"

El Encanto took one measured step after another, moving carefully toward the bull, his muleta wiping the ground like a cloth broom. "Eh hayyy toro!" he challenged the bull to charge. Suddenly, from twenty yards away the bull charged. The scenario to Chester was dreamlike. It was as though a Neanderthal cave painting had come to life. El Encanto calmly received the charge, swinging the muleta an inch in

41

front of the bull's snout, leading him with a piece of cloth. Chester felt perspiration dampen his armpits as he tilted the bottle up for a nervous sip. He turned to offer the bottle to his companion, but she refused with a shake of her head, her eyes glistening, the corners of her mouth wet.

El Encanto led the bull through a series of interwoven passes and literally hypnotized the bull to a wrenching stop by artfully jerking the cloth from the bull's vision and standing stone still just out of his range of vision. He thought she was saying a prayer at first. "I love this thing of the bulls, I love this, all of it." Again, El Encanto allowed the bull to experience the illusion of having achieved an attack and then withdrew the object that the bull was charging. After the fifth charge, El Encanto called softly to Chester.

"Chester, my friend, don't drink all the cognac, I will need some when this done."

The bull no longer needed encouragement to charge. He turned on a dime and charged again and again. El Encanto passed him on the right, on the left, controlling the direction of the charges with steel wrists. Chester started writing his bullfight novel from behind the olive tree.

It was not five o'clock in the afternoon, as the story is traditionally told, but three a.m. on a moonlight night somewhere in a pasture outside the city of Valencia. He felt her move before he fully understood what had happened. The bull had caught El Encanto squarely between the horns, in the cradle, and tossed him and was stabbing the ground as El Encanto rolled away. Blanca snatched the muleta from the ground and waved it to distract the bull.

"Hayyy toro! Eh hayyy toro!" She took off both shoes and threw them at the bull as Pepe, Tito and Manuel flashed their capes to add to the distraction. The bull turned toward Blanca, pounded the ground twice with his hooves and charged. From his perspective the bull seemed to be charging straight at him. Video images of fire engines with horns flashed through his head. The woman placed her left hand on her hip and leaned into the bull's charge by stepping forward a half step and at the same time, capturing the bull's off eye attention with a gentle sway of the muleta. The visual effect was of one leaning slightly forward to open a garden gate. "Ole's" erupted from the cuadrilla. Three times she led the bull past her with right handed naturales before El Encanto retrieved the muleta and let the bull away with a series of side-to-side motions of the cloth, a movement called "ki kiri ki".

She walked toward the tree as though she were floating. Chester felt uncomfortable, vaguely ashamed. He was the only one who had not made an effort to come to El Encanto's aid. El Encanto forced the bull to make a final charge and slowly backed away from him, leaving the bull tired and frustrated.

Yes, it was three a.m. and the fight was over and the men and the woman who had saved the matador's life slowly faded from the field of battle, ghostly figures. They were silent, reloading the capes, until they started the trip back to the city.

"Chester, there is more cognac, no?"

He handed the bottle to the bullfighter, still feeling vaguely ill at ease. Manuel looked over the front seat, admiration in his eyes. "You were in good form, matador."

"And what of this one?" Ernesto Suares asked, curling his arm around Blanca Cruz-Espana's neck. The men released three choruses of Ole's in a measured rhythm. The woman smiled her acknowledgement of the cheers and then turned to the matador, pouting a fresh coat of lipstick at him.

"Ernesto, I lost my shoes back there, my good ones."

"Don't worry, Blanca, we will buy you many shoes, many more." El Encanto kissed the woman, more a kiss of friendship than passion and then turned to Chester and whispered, "You see how it is, my friend, to be in the arena with the bull can do more to inspire fear than bravery."

"I hear that," Chester responded.

tall and throw the basketball through the basket, hah hah, hah, hah, or they run very, very fast, no?''

"I understand that. And if poor people are the same everywhere, then why didn't you go into boxing or learn how to play soccer. Why the corrida?''

El Encanto, sprawled out on Chester's rickety bed, a large glass of cognac encased between his hands. "Ahhhh, Chester, my friend. You ask such difficult questions . . .''

"Why the corrida, El Encanto, why not soccer?''

He had discovered, after many hours, that it was best to drive on Ernesto Suares, if he wanted something. There was the strong possibility of getting what he wanted and more. The bullfighter took a long, thoughtful sip from his glass and stared out of the window for a few moments.

"Chester, my friend, I don't know if I can say this right in Ingles.''

"Say it in Spanish then.''

Once again the bullfighter took a sip from his glass and stared out of the window before answering. His expression was far away, dreamy and his Spanish was slurred. Chester listened closely, translating in his mind. "You must understand, my friend, that the Spanish are the Africans of Europe, the Portuguese, even more so, but of course you will find many people who disagree with this. Nevertheless, it is true.

"The Moors of Africa colonized our land for almost eight-hundred years and they left us the legacy of the corrida, of the bullfight. Once again, there are many who would deny this because they do not like to admit how much of our culture comes from the Moorish times, from Africa.'' Chester straightened up in his chair, stunned by what he was hearing.

"I think this is one of the reasons why many Spanish people hate the Gypsies, because they are a reminder of the Moors.''

"The Gypsies?''

47

"Yes, the Gypsies. The Gypsies come from Egypt, from Africa, and there are many who we do not like." El Encanto paused for a drink. "I am Gitano, Gypsy, on both sides of my family, my grandparents."

"But what does this have to do with your becoming a bullfighter?"

Ernesto Suares stared into Chester's eyes. "To become a bullfighter, my friend, is to become a priest, because the bullfight is a religion. And I became a priest. I had no choice. It was my calling."

"Ernesto, I must be honest with you. I never heard anything about the bullfight being a religion, explain that to me."

El Encanto sat up quickly, spilling some of his cognac. "Yes, of course, it is a religion. We are priests, the matadors. And the public worships in the arena. They come, at five o'clock in the afternoon, to witness the ritual, to see the sacrifice, to watch the priests, to determine if we are doing our work as well as possible."

Chester mentally erased six pages of bullshit that he had written three days before. "I don't understand, where is the African religious connection?"

"Don't you see, Chester, religion is Africa and Africa is religion. Wherever Africa goes it takes religion. This is the greatest thing that the African people have brought to the world. Not just religion, but spirituality. The corrida is African at its core. It offers a powerful male symbol, the bull, with horns and cojones...." They both smiled. "And they ask a cute little fellow, like me, hairless, with small cojones, to stick a knife into this symbol, to do something that they would be afraid to do. But first, before that, they ask me to flirt with death, using only a little piece of cloth, to do something that they are not spiritually qualified to do. Some of us are sad about what we do, like Manolete and some others, but others rejoice. Sometimes, I rejoice in what I do, but often I do not rejoice. I am afraid of what I must do and I cannot stand to take another animal's life. After all, are we not all animals?''

The story was shaping up and the day of El Encanto's upcoming debut in the city of Seville occupied Chester's mind. ''Matador, Ernesto, El Encanto, pal, when are you going to start training, warming up for your coming fight. It's only about three weeks away?''

Ernesto, the bullfighter, flopped over on his stomach to get a better look at the soaps and announced, ''Chester, you don't understand, my friend, you cannot become as strong as a bull. You cannot think like one, because they are very smart. Do you know that the bull I fought, that *we* fought, Blanca and I, will probably kill someone in the ring because we made him aware of what the difference is, between man and a piece of cloth? Yes, the bulls are much smarter than us. They never forget. We forget all the time, that is when we are most often gored. Not by the bulls, but by people like ourselves, who want more of us than we can give. They are desperate for salvation and they want my blood to cleanse them.

''I have spoken to men from Africa about The Religion and it's manifestations in the world. They gave me much interesting information concerning sacrifices and how everything must balance out.''

''But still, man, don't you have to practice killing the bull, aiming for the right spot n' shit?''

''Chester, my friend, it is my will that kills the bull, nothing else. Jogging would only tire me out and would not prepare me for the supreme effort involved in killing anything. They say Carnacerito de Mexico used to fuck every afternoon at noon. It was like a ritual with him. We might call him an Oshun priest, a love priest. The college girls loved him to death, literally.''

"And what kind of priest are you?"

"I am a negligent priest. I am human, I didn't pray that my ancestors would make me what I am. I have nothing to do with it. Why do you think they call me El Encanto, the enchanted one?''

Chester stood at the foot of the bed, staring down on El Encanto's sleeping body. He was struck by the Christlike look of the man. It wasn't European northern. It was African Southern. He could've been a pharaoh, an Egyptian God. He was snoring gently and to cement his relationship to immortality, he turned slightly to his left and released a muted stream of farts. Chester smiled at him. ''Yeah, this is the way I like my priests, funky armpits, half drunk and wise.''

Chapter 6

The first fight of the season for El Encanto was a complete disaster. It was in the city of Seville, a deep southern Spanish city, that took great pride in its aficion, in the knowledge they had of the bullfight. They knew the difference between a man pretending to work close to the bull and one who was doing the tricks. El Encanto's attempt to conceal his fear was tragic. He jumped back from the bull whenever possible, or tried to blind the animal by pushing the cape into his eyes. He was frightened, scared and at the end, whistled out of the bullring. Chester raced to the hotel, expecting to find El Encanto in tears, ashamed for having shown such cowardice in the ring.

Chester opened the door to a roomful of people having a party. El Encanto raced over to him, a Danish blonde in tow. "Ahhh, Chester, you made it."

Chester couldn't contain his surprise. "You know, frankly, I thought you'd be up here in your room, crying your eyes out." El Encanto looked into Chester's face, turned to the girl and whooped with laughter.

"Chester, my friend, this is not American baseball. I do not go to the locker room and kick the drinking fountain and hurt my toe. Or start a fight with someone. I rejoice because I have gone into the bullring with an animal who could destroy me with one inch of his horn. Do you know how many men have left the bullring without his cajones? It is always possible."

"But what about the crowd, the feelings?"

"The crowd is fickle and never really knows what it wants. They go on to ask others to give more than they have, while I eat, drink and make love."

Ernesto Suares made one of his characteristic turns and spoke over his shoulder as he made his way into the heart of the scene. "Come into this life, my friend, because we can be certain that we will always leave it. We will never be kept waiting in a line for life to end."

Cadiz was a repeat of Seville. El Encanto was fighting through the southern part of the country and the people took great pride in their knowledge of sherries and the bullfight. Chester had the misfortune of having a contraberrara seat next to a quartet of scotch-soaked American tourists who were determined, because they had seen him talking to El Encanto, to have him give them a blow by blow description of what was happening.

"You're an American, aren't you?" He felt tempted to ignore them, but realized it wouldn't be possible. They were being thrown together by circumstances beyond his control.

"Uhhh, yeah, I guess you could call me that."

"How's about a lil' drink?"

"Sorry, wine gives me an earache."

One of the tourists, a large framed blonde guy, with a broken nose, leaned closer to say, "No wine in these

52

wineskins, pal. They're filled with White Horse scotch."
Chester considered the offer. What the hell, scotch is scotch.
White Horse scotch? There were three men fighting: Carlos
Fuentos, "El Gallo," Roberto Vidal, "Hijo do la Frontera,"
and Ernesto Suares, "El Encanto." And the bulls were from
the ranch of the noted breeder, the Duke of Manteno y
Congresso.

Chester could see, after the first five minutes, that El
Encanto was in for a rough afternoon and so was he.
"What're they gonna do, the horses with the pads on, and
those guys with the spears." Chester shook his head in
disbelief. Who would pay good money to see a spectacle that
they didn't know the first thing about? The answer was easy:
American tourists. He looked the quartet over carefully.
They're probably suburbanites who've saved money for a
year to come to Spain, thinking that Spain was Mexico and
that Cadiz was Tijuana, with all due respect to Tijuana and
Mexico.

And now here they are, drunk and semi-disorderly,
boisterous, white, ugly. He was surprised to find himself
thinking in such clearly racial terms, but it was impossible
not to. The ugly American was the rule, not the exception,
and they were usually Anglo.

"Well, the men on the padded horses are called picadores
and their job is to pic the bull."

"Pic the bull? How do they do that? Awright, Jim, go easy,
we don't want to run out before this thing is over."

"Just watch, you'll see how they pic the bull, just watch."

The first bull, a roan colored giant with horns that looked
like antlers, slammed into one of the picadores. Chester
recognized Manuel, one of the men from the moonlight
excursion, as the picador. He shot the pearlike lance into
the bull's hump and bore down. One of the American women
screamed and turned away from the sight of the blood running

53

out of the wound. The two men suddenly seemed a little less drunk. Interesting, the effect that blood has on people. Chester decided to offer a running commentary, to prevent the tourists from asking him dumb questions at crucial moments. "Remember, everything that's done to the bull, from the minute he runs into the ring, is preparation for his death." He felt good, excited by his knowledge of what was happening. "The man on the padded horse pics, sticks his lance into the bull's hump so that he'll be weakened, so that when the bullfighter reaches the moment of truth..."

"Ahhhh, yeahhhh, the moment of truth. Hemingway wrote about that."

"Right. The bull's head would be too high for the bullfighter to go over the horns if he wasn't weakened. You've got to remember, a bull can toss a car over, that's how strong they are." The woman who had screamed was sobbing softly, afraid to look but peeking between her fingers so as not to miss anything.

"Okay, now the padded horses are out. What're those guys going to do with those sticks?"

"The sticks are called bandarillas and once upon a time, according to some authorities, they were used to correct hooking defects in the bull. If the bull hooked to the left, for example, a good bandarillero could stick the sticks in on the right side to correct that tendency. Nowadays, they just seem to plunge the sticks in and run." He accepted the bota wineskin filled with scotch without another word, turned it up for a full mouthful. The first bull, the roan-colored monster, was called Isabella and it belonged to Ernesto Suares, El Encanto.

During the course of his running commentary, Chester had kept his eyes on El Encanto. He had performed quite well, luring the bull away from Manuel's expert pic, after two, with chiculinas antiguas. The crowd Ole'd and applauded.

54

They seldom saw chicuelinas antiguas performed. Tito and Pepe placed bandarillos. They ran the quarter circle and plunged the sticks into the bull's hump. The work was done quickly, efficiently.

"Those babies don't play, do they?" the one they called Jim announced.

And now the faena, the third act that sets the scene for the last act. Ernesto Suares made the formal request for a change of acts, from the part of the bandarillas, to the faena, the close work with the muleta. The president of the arena granted his request for the change with a wave of his handkerchief. El Encanto bowed and made a stiff-legged walk to where Chester was sitting. He held the muleta and sword in his left hand and held his montera up to Chester, saluting him and offering the bull to him. The Americans were impressed. The bullfighter was dedicating a bull to them. Chester had to snatch the bullfighter's hat away from Jim's wife when he turned his back and tossed it up to him.

"Sorry, lady, this one's for me."

Ernesto flashed an ultra-confident smile at Chester and then at the crowd and strode boldly out into the center of the ring, to flirt with death, to meet his destiny. Chester felt like crying, knowing behind the brave facade, that El Encanto was close to peeing on himself with fear. The Duke of Manteno y Congresso bull, who had not adopted a querencia, stared at the man walking slowly toward him. The bull seemed to blink with delighted surprise, "Ahhhh, now, after I've been jabbed with a spear and I've had little barbed sticks stuck in my muscles, I have a chance to do some damage." Chester said a silent prayer. "God in Heaven, I hope it's not that bull he played with in that pasture that night."

The bull raced past El Encanto and snatched the muleta from his hands. Even the Americans laughed at the sight of the bull racing around the arena with the bullfighter's cape on his left horn. El Encanto chased the bull for a few futile steps, looking for all the world like a man who had just missed the last bus, and then he stopped, put his hands on his hips and cursed. The pantomime was hilarious. One of the peones raced out and snatched the muleta from the bull's horn, risking his life, while another one of El Encanto's cuadrilla gave him a fresh cape. The bull felt bolder now, his horn had struck something and he knew that there was more to come.

El Encanto cited the bull from twenty yards away and when he charged, he whirled around with a pass that was called a molinete.

"What was that?"

"He just did a pass that was called a molinete. It's like the man spinning a top around the bull's horns. And the one he's doing now is called a natural en redondo." Chester felt himself floating up from his seat with the rest of the members of the audience, to applaud the cape work of a master. El Encanto positioned the bull in place with a series of passes and finished it off with a beautiful remate, the whipping of the cape in front of the bull's face that will sometimes cause the bull to look as though he had been paralyzed. Once again, the aficion was driven to its feet by the man's artistry.

Chester scribbled a random line in his head. *El Encanto had found himself, he had created a sense of connection between himself and one of nature's most elaborate concoctions, the species of Bos Africanus.* Thirty seconds later, he was silently erasing all that he had written. El Encanto was fucking up royally. The bull brushed into him when he tried to make a pass that was not right for the bull, and sprawled on the sand, looking exactly like a commuter who had missed his bus. For a moment, the crowd was too shocked to laugh. And when they did laugh, it was filled with whistles, boos (from the suddenly knowledgeable

56

Americans) and obscene remarks.

"This is Cadiz, 'El Asshole,' and we know what the corrida is. Get up off your ass."

Chester snatched the wine bag from his neighbors and spilled a water glass of scotch down his gullet. Damn!

El Encanto stood up and brushed himself off, but the magic was gone. He was just an ordinary man making an effort to do something that most of the men (and some of the women) had thought about doing but didn't have the courage to do. Chester didn't have to explain the eight inept attempts El Encanto made to try to kill the bull.

"That poor guy's having a hard time trying to slaughter that critter, ain't he?"

The aficion cursed El Encanto's origins, his father's lack of consideration for the rest of the world by contributing his genes for such a specimen, his mother's arrogance for carrying such an awful fetus in her womb for so long and other Spanish curses of southern origin. One of the spectators, obviously expecting a fiasco from El Encanto, tossed a cap pistol into the ring. The implication was obvious. It you can't kill it with a sword, shoot it.

Finally, after the bull had collapsed from loss of blood and fatigue, El Encanto was able to take the descabello sword and sever his spinal cord. The brave bull from the finca Manteno had succumbed to the inept bullfighter from Valencia.

The crowd booed and whistled for ten minutes. And this was only the first bull for El Encanto, he had one more to go. What made the whole thing even worse was the bullfights that Carlos Fuentes, "El Gallo," and Roberto Vidal, "Hijo de la Frontera," put together. Between the two of them, they flashed capes, made visual impressions, appealed to a media crowd. Most of the older aficionados hated the showboat stuff, the bullfighting a la disco. They wanted "classical

57

bullfighting," like authentic African-American jazz, stuff with stuff in it. They had counted on El Encanto to bring them that, the profound meaning of the sacrifice. But, today he had failed them. Some of them understood and stood to applaud his appearance. It was how deep they felt about him. Most of the people didn't understand and they berated him, they accused him of taking their money and not giving them any *emoción*. They were strong about that. They needed emoción. Emoción was not supplied by the TV. Somebody else's wife, a trip to the movies, or the porno houses. Emoción was caused in the bullring and El Encanto had let them down.

The aficion, those members of the public who really knew and understood the corrida, the meaning of life and death, smiled as El Encanto tried to escape from the bullring. They hovered over him like angels and he was never certain whether they wanted him to live or die.

Chester sipped a glass of grapefruit juice in the hotel dining room the next morning, waiting for El Encanto to show his face. Jerez de la Frontera, Malega and Granada were still in front of them, how in the fuck could he begin to fuck up so soon?

El Encanto sipped his orange juice, signed autographs, tried to explain to Chester what disgrace meant. "It means nothing to me, Chester. I simply go to meet the bulls, hoping that the Orisa will touch my dreams."

"Orisa? What the fuck are you talking about man. What the hell do your ancestors have to do with you doing well in the arena?"

"Chester, my friend, I told you, my grandparents on both sides are Gypsies, we believe in our ancestors. If it is not this time, it will be the next time. Where is the next fight, Jerez de la Frontera? They have a wonderful sherry there. Perhaps I shall do better."

58

Chester backed away, recognizing the danger zones. Don't get too involved with this motherfucker. He's off.

Jerez de la Frontera: "The bulls were not the best."

Malaga: "There were too many there with mirrors. Did you see how the lights were flashing from the arena?"

Granada: "Well, what can you expect in Granada? They grow excellent marijuana, but the bulls are cold, too willing to kill."

Jaen: "I always hated Jaen, too many virgins."

And so on.

He had the most logical excuses for every bad showing. "The bulls are not as intelligent as they used to be." Chester had to constantly hold himself in check. Just get the facts and write. Don't try to influence this mad man; that he ought to show some integrity. But then he reasoned, who in the hell can talk about integrity when a man is risking his life every time he goes to work?

I'd be the last one.

And they continued slugging their way around Spain. The promoters were hostile, the public was hostile, but they had to see this magician who could make you feel something you'd never felt before.

It happened in the city of Leon. Chester placed his elbows on the contraberrara rail, slightly hung over from the night of boozing with El Encanto. He was feeling irritable about everything: traveling, the crowds, the fly by night atmosphere, El Encanto's cowardice. And then it happened.

El Encanto started it by kneeling in front of the gate where the bulls run into the ring. They shoot into the arena like trains, some of the bulls. The bull shot out of the gate and made straight for El Encanto. El Encanto had pulled the same maneuver in another ring and the bull had bowled him over, barely missing his eye with the left horn. This time it was different. He swirled the cape at just the precise moment the bull was driving at his head and deflected the charge. He was controlling the fight from the beginning. He offered the lure of the large cape, and when he whirled the cape in front of the bull's nose like a flag, so slowly that it seemed to melt, they screamed. El Encanto was giving them the old-fashioned corrida, something fitted with arrogance and disdain. He took the muleta and made passes that looked as though they were carvings. He planted his feet together in the sand and led the bull around and around his body, working closer to the horns with every turn.

Some of the more squeamish types were screaming. They were long drawn out screams. He had linked them to the possibility of death. And primeval urges and feelings made them scream. Chester stood, screaming with all the others. El Encanto was truly being El Encanto, the enchanted one. His face and body seemed to glow during the fight. At one point, pausing in the middle of a series of passes, he looked around the arena and asked, ''Am I not the greatest matador in the whole world?'' The crowds lavish applause answered the question. The moment of truth, which sometimes lingered an hour for some, was only a moment on this occasion.

El Encanto sighted down the length of his sword, neatly used the muleta in his left hand to lead the bull past his right thigh and crossed his arms, placing the sword dead in the center of the bull's neck. The sword sank down between the shoulder bones, cutting the heart muscle, causing the bull to hemorrhage and keel over almost immediately. The crowd went wild. This is what they had come to experience. El Encanto was given a triumphant clockwise walk around the bullring. People threw flowers, wineskins, hats, shoes and from one anonymous admirer, a pair of black lace panties. El Encanto sniffed into the crotch of the panties and pantomimed to the crowd that he recognized the scent.

The crowd loved it.

They awarded him the ears and tail of the bull and sang his praises. The sun seemed to glitter in the sky above his head. He was the bravest and the best.

After the fight and people slapping him on the back, Chester found El Encanto in his hotel suite, a beautiful woman on each arm, a cigar sticking out of his mouth, laughing, having a good time. Chester strolled around the room, picking up the vibes. How could someone go from being a complete nothing one day, to being a god the following Sunday? He decided to put the question to Ernesto Suares. To make it legitimate, he pulled a note pad and pen out. "Ernesto, let me speak with you for a moment."

"Chester, my friend, let me introduce you to my two friends. On my left is Marianna and Julieta is on my right. They saw the fantastic fight I made this afternoon." Chester nodded pleasantly, the last thing he wanted was fresh flesh. He had run through an economy-sized box of condoms over the course of the past month, simply dealing the El Encantos cast offs and rejects. No, it wasn't pussy he needed. It was information. He wanted to know what it felt like to go from nothing to something. El Encanto dismissed the ladies. "Go, eat, get fat. We'll look at your naked bodies later." He linked his arm through Chester's arm and led him through the crowd to a secluded sofa. "Now then, my friend, what do you want to know?"

"I want to know how it feels to be considered a brave man, to be admired, to know that you have accomplished something that few other men would even dare attempt?"

Ernesto Suares puffed on his cigar and blew rings to the ceiling. "How does one feel when one is mounted on the hips of a beautiful woman?"

"You mean you feel a sensual pleasure?"

"More than that."

Chester couldn't tell if Ernesto was putting him on or not.

"What else happens?"

"Chester, what can I say to you. One day I am the villain and the next day I am a hero, but you must understand, I am always me."

Chester probed, anxious to find out something about a layer of feeling that he'd never been exposed to. "I understand that, Ernesto. I understand that you are always you, but how does that explain what happened today? You seemed to be transformed, to become someone else. You went beyond yourself. How can you explain that?"

"I cannot explain. It is what it is. I feel like an instrument that some higher power is using. It's like your dick, Chester, you know?"

"My dick? What're you talking about?"

"You cannot say when you are with a lovely woman, that you are in control of your dick. She controls it, she stirs the blood in it. She brings it up. That is something of what happens with me and the bulls."

"That's what happened to you today?"

"The bulls were formidable."

"But the bulls in Seville and Cadiz and Lorca and Santiago de Compostela were extraordinary, too."

"Yes, you are right, but they were not inspiring to me."

People were closing in on them. They wanted El Encanto. They wanted to talk with him, listen to him, look into his eyes, fuck him, be with him. Ernesto Suares leaned close to whisper into Chester's ear. "Chester, my friend, Marianna and Julieta are, how you say, freaks. You want to . . . ?"

Chester nodded no politely and eased off the sofa. It was time to get back to the drawing board, to try to deal honestly with the psyche of a man who seemed to be almost mystical, when he wasn't overwhelmed by fear.

The triumph of Leon was not repeated in Burgos, or Bilbao. Chester stood in place, staring down into the Bilbao bullring, trying to figure out why El Encanto couldn't seem to get untracked. He shook his head, unable to believe his eyes. Two weeks before, in Leon, he had had people screaming and crying with emotional outbursts; now some of the same people who had journeyed from Leon to experience what they could never normally feel, were throwing their cushions into the bullring, disgusted. He just couldn't understand it. The bulls were small, manageable, but El Encanto could do nothing with them. His outrageous cowardice made the people angry. He popped into the limo taking them back to the Hotel Bilbao. Ernesto Suares was pouring himself a glass of cognac from the rear seat tray.

"Ahhh, Chester, my friend. After a bad day, a good cognac, after a good day, a good cognac." He shared a drink as the driver eased through the hostile crowd outside the bullring. Several people spat on the window. El Encanto quickly powered the window down and spat a mouthful of cognac out at the people who had spat. Chester smiled at his action.

"Careful, Ernesto, my friend, we don't want to waste good cognac on the wrong people."

"You are absolutely right, my friend, absolutely right." Chester decided to skip his usual post bullfight questions. He felt slightly burned out. How to explain, how a man will fight bulls that look like cathedrals one day and shy away from animals that looked like large donkeys, the next.

"Chester," Ernesto turned to him with a serious look in his eyes, "did you see how the second bull, the one called Cascabel, looked at me?"

"I couldn't really see his eyes that well from where I was sitting."

"Well, then, of course, you could not hear him speak to me either."

"The bull spoke to you?"

"Yes, he said, 'Ernesto, I'm going to pluck your balls from between your legs like grapes.'"

"The bull said that to you?"

"Yes, above the noise of the crowd, above everything."

Chester slumped back in his seat. "Mmmmm, not only is he scared to death, now he's beginning to lose his mind." And the Feria de San Fermin, the running of the bulls was the next stop. The Feria de San Fermin meant a nonstop party for six days and nights, complete with firecrackers and bulls from the most famous bull ranches in Spain. "If he's hallucinating now, no telling what's going to happen to him in Pamplona." Pamplona was almost a throwback to medieval times, with its festival flavor.

After three days and nights of nonstop eating, drinking and acting crazy, Chester felt the need for a break. He hired a taxi and had the driver take him to the outskirts of the city for a half-hour of silence. The driver wandered off to take a leak and smoke a cigarette as Chester sprawled on a grassy place, trying to make a decision. I can see what this is going to lead to. Nada. The man is a loser. He's a charming loser, but still a loser. Chester had held out hope, since the miraculous demonstration of courage and art in the bullfight at Leon; that Ernesto Suares, El Encanto, would somehow get a grip on himself and pull the miracle off again. But it hadn't happened. In fight after fight, he found new ways to disgrace himself.

"So I had to piss, what could I do?"

"They didn't know. They only thought that my pants were becoming wet from perspiration."

"Ernesto, you ever met anyone who could sweat between his legs so profusely, that it would wet the area between his thighs?"

"What is this word you use, pro-luze-lee?"

"That's okay, Ernesto, don't sweat it."

He strolled back to the car, his mouth dry and salty from salted shrimp and beer, cognac and coffee, anchovies and white wine, sherry and paella. He was sleepy, but there was no place to sleep in Pamplona. He had tried to seclude himself in one of the city's hundreds of churches, to take a nap on a back pew but that didn't work either. The festival was everywhere.

"Where to now, Señor?"

"Back to the madhouse, where else?"

"Back to where, Señor?"

"Back to town. Let's go back to town." The decision reached, turning a curve in the road. I've had enough of this. I have all the material I could use in two lifetimes, why should I continue to abuse myself with this maniac? I'll split tomorrow afternoon, after his fight.

The San Fermin bullfights were the high point of the festival. Thousands of people would fill the arena, the best bulls and hopefully, the best men would fight each other. Yeah, I'll wait 'til after the fight is over on Sunday and then I'll split. No sense upsetting the dude before time. He had acquired a portable typewriter, learned how to type with both forefingers and sent a few queries off to prospective publishers. But beyond that, he had become a friend of El Encanto and that was a talent that required much more than the use of forefingers.

He was becoming sick and tired of being associated with El Encanto, the one that some people had punned into El Cobarde, the coward. He felt for the man but was beginning to lose his sympathy.

"Ernesto, if you're that goddamned scared of the bulls, then why don't you leave it alone, go into tap dancing, or shoe repairing, or whatever. Why bullfighting?"

"Chester, my friend, as I have told you many times, I did not chose the bulls, the bulls chose me."

Chapter 7

It took four whiskey sours for him to permit himself to be stuffed into the sick banderillos suit of lights. "Whooaaaa! hold on here, don't you think people will know that I'm not Tito?"

El Encanto, the supreme ironist, smiled. "They will not know if you do not hold your head up proudly, the way I do. No one pays any attention to the banderillo. They are just men who perform an outdated function. She is like your prostate gland."

"She? She who?"

"The man who places the sticks in the bull's hump. Do it well and people will applaud. Do it badly and they will hardly notice. One must be extraordinary or very ordinary to be noticed in the bullfight." Ernesto sounded casual about his knowledge, but Chester knew, as off hand as he was, that El Encanto was a superb crowd psychologist.

"So now what do I do when the bull charges me?"

"You have a few choices. You can stand absolutely still, until the bull notices you and charges. You fake to your left or right as he goes past you put the sticks in."

"That doesn't sound too hard." Cushioned by gallons of burgundy, as they talked, danced in circles in the city's squares, the people drank as they had breakfast, lunch, the evening meal. Some people seemed grapelike, wine-intoxicated from the best wines. Life was lush for them, they were celebrities or peasants, for a moment. They were people enjoying themselves.

Reports of uninhibited behavior were much less prevalent than years gone by. AIDS stopped a lot of the sexual Pamplona from happening, but it seemed to have internalized something. People gathered around bonfires in orgy circles, crying for the injustices that all sensitive people felt. They were as much into pure fucking as anyone, but now it was no longer safe, and they felt that it was man-created, and they all had the blues about it. They felt that man had finally outdone himself. He had created the last obstacle to lovemaking. And he was ashamed. He had destroyed lakes, streams, rivers, ponds, oceans; he had made millions of acres of ground into stone wall, filled the air with deadly vapors, created a deathly food supply, smothered the life from himself. And then he put a damper on fucking. It was enough to cry about it and they did, swaying around the fire.

"What's the other way, Ernesto, for putting the sticks in?" Chester felt impatient with Ernesto, sprawled on the bed with a *zaftig* blonde from Malibu, California, who had come to Spain to get herself a bullfighter. And she was getting him. And she was rich. And El Encanto was enchanted.

"Ernesto, buddy, would you hold off for just a minute and tell me what I'm supposed to do?" He was slightly pissed. And half high and beginning to wonder if being for real was all that it's cracked up to be. Why go into the bullring? Ernesto deflected the blonde's tongue and spoke from the corners of his mouth. She wasn't much on talking but she loved to kiss.

"Chester, my friend, go into the ring, make a li'l quarter circle and stick the sticks in the bull as he goes by."

"That simple, huh?"

"Yes, that simple. The only thing one has to do is collect the sweat from one's balls to wrap around the shit that is pouring from one's loose bowels because one is scared into shitting, knowing that you are on the naked ground with a naked enemy, one who has no respect or regard for your race, your religion, your color, your name, your sex, nothing, nada. The bull has an incredible sense of territory. The Earth belongs to him and you are a threat. Comprende?"

Chester stared down at El Encanto, sprawled on the bed, the blonde had pulled his dick out of his shorts and was playing around with it, a little like a little girl with a limp doll that was coming to life. He was supposed to be getting dressed for the corrida, they only had an hour. While the other members of the cuadrilla went about the business of preparation, avoiding the sight of El Encanto and the blonde, Chester stared at the spectacle, regretting that he had foolishly agreed to participate in his corrida as a substitute member of the cuadrilla. He turned away from the sight of the blonde and the bullfighter enjoying each other and sewed his decision up.

"Nawww, it wouldn't make a lot of sense to continue to hang out with you, you don't take yourself seriously."

Chapter 8

Chester woke up screaming a half dozen times, on the train from Pamplona to Alicante, from the northwest of Spain to the southeast. Inside one of the dreams that caused him to scream, a stroboscopic bull was racing toward him. The picture of Leger's "Nude Descending a Staircase" offered the perfect analogy. The bull's horns seemed to detach themselves from the bull's head and plunge at him, and then the eyes, the huge hump, the morillo and finally the entire bulk of the beast. He could only stand there, screaming, two banderillas held above his head, screaming, screaming...WHAT THE FUCK AM I 'SPOSED TO DO WITH THESE GODDAMNED STICKS?

Inside another version of the dream, the bull was standing a yard away from him, just standing there, chewing on a few stray pieces of straw, winking at him, telling him, "In a minute, as soon as I finish eatin' these pieces of straw, I'm gonna come over there 'n tear your ass up."

In all the dreams, the bull, the beast, was the dominant figure. He had never dreamed of a bull before, but now he couldn't get the horrible picture of the bull out of his dreams. He had gone into the ring at Pamplona. He had put his ass on the line and survived. He knew a lot more, based on that one foolish move, than most of his readers would ever know.

The bullfight, the corrida, that El Encanto had put together for his first bull, El Rey, had been a grand disaster. The bull raced into the arena, a superb member of his species. He had faced the picadores and come away undiminished, angry. He had tried to catch a "sleeping banderillero" and had failed. He roared into the faena, full of fire and intelligence.

The aficion, those few people in the crowd who recognized the nobility of the bull, looked forward to a superb demonstration of what the combination of superior man and superb bull could pull together. El Encanto, for whatever reasons, disappointed them. He started backing away from the bull during the opening veronicas, and stepped into sheer dodging when he arrived at the faena. Many of the aficion, nourished on Manolete, Giron, Procuna (during his best moments), Arruza, simply cried at the spectacle of this fool making a mockery of a holy event.

El Rey, "the king", had been exceptionally gracious to El Encanto. He had offered charges. No gratuitous hooking, no uneven defects or genetic character. There were critics who would've call him a perfect bull. For El Encanto, he had been a disaster. He had shown all of the traits that honest bullfighters looked for: a sincere charge, beautiful horn formation, a desire for fighting. Many of the aficion thought he deserved the indulto (the pardon) halfway through El Encanto's sloppy faena. This was clearly a case of the bull being superior to the man.

Chester stood behind the barrera, groaning from the semi-hangover that always accompanied him when he was with

El Encanto. Even he felt that he could've done a better job with El Rey than El Encanto had done. My lord in heaven, if ever a bullfighter wanted to fight the perfect bull, El Rey is the bull. Ten thousand Spaniards agreed with him. But El Encanto didn't agree. He resisted any effort to do an honest treatment of the bull. And the aficion hated him for it. One section of the audience, more drunk than any of the other sections, spontaneously started singing, "El Cobade", the coward, who faces the bulls and has no balls. El Encanto weathered the protests, he even smiled through them.

"We have one more bull, Chester, my friend, and then we can return to our normal lives."

"Ojos Negros" was El Encanto's final bull and Chester had the strangest notion that someone had played a trick on them. Ojos Negros, black eyes, was obviously a mutant from the ranch. He was large, ungainly, his horns unevenly matched, his general appearance esthetically displeasing. Many of those who had cried, now groaned.

"Chester, my friend, this is the one you will place the first pair of sticks in, suerte!"

"In this one?"

"There are no others."

Chester felt his heart thumping so hard he thought he was about to have a heart attack. Ojos Negros made a savage attack on the padding of the picadore's horse. El Encanto encouraged the picador to assassinate the bull by placing the pics behind the hump, into the spine, to paralyze its savagery. The whistles, boos and cushions prevented the picador from completing his dirty work, forcing him to leave the ring. El Encanto used the pass called *chicuelina* to perform the quiet, to lure the bull away from his attack on the padded horse. He performed the chicuelinas so effortlessly that the cape seemed to be a part of him, a gracefully ambulating creature who led the bull from one side of his body to the other. The crowd applauded his cape work, but there were scattered whistles, holdovers from his previous bull. El Encanto wedged himself through the buladero, into the callejon, a small, cold, determined smile on his face.

"This is a beautiful bull, my friend, beautiful. Go and see for yourself."

Manuel and Tito, the other members of the cuadrilla trotted out into the arena to do their job, to place the banderillos. Manuel whispered to Chester, "Watch me first, it is simple, the sticks." Chester watched closely, the geometry of running a quarter pattern until the intersection of man and bull occurred, the man raising his arms with the sticks and plunging them into the bull's hump as he shot past. Everything seems to be directed at that hump. Manuel made a neat evasion from the bull's line of vision, his escape aided by Tito's distracting the bull with a shout, "Heyy toro!" He trotted over to the barrera for his cape and back to Chester's side.

"Now, Chester, do exactly as I did. Don't worry about anything, we will be nearby to help you." Chester took a wild-eyed look around the bullring. The place seemed to be filled with lunatics, mad men and women. Who was it that said that the bull is not the monster in the arena, the crowd is. He heard several people shout, "Mira! Un Negro!," "Look a Black!" as he felt his feet propel him into the quartering run that Manuel had shown him. The bull seemed to jerk his head around, catching sight of the new threat. Chester's knees trembled, his eyes suddenly felt scratchy, as though he had sand in them and his heart had kicked into a faster rhythm.

"Oh my gawd! Here he comes!"

The urge for survival forced him to make the quartering run, to meet the bull at the intersection. He practically threw one of the banderillas into the bull's hump as he ran past.

The crowd gave him a good-natured hand as he trotted back to the barrera, to safety, still holding a banderilla. They knew that he wasn't one of the regular members of the cuadrilla, and that caused them to grant him a little artistic license. El Encanto embraced him in the callejo. "That was very good, Chester, my friend. Very good." Chester's teeth were chattering so hard from tension that he couldn't say anything. Damn, I'm thirsty, he thought.

El Encanto marched to the center of the ring while Tito distracted the bull. He stood in the center of the ring for a moment and then made a slow turn with his montera in his right hand, dedicating the bull to the unruly crowd.

"To you, bastards," he said under his breath. And then he planted both feet inside his montera and stood there, as straight as a pole. Manuel lured the bull into a position that made it possible for the bull to see El Encanto and took up a supporting position.

"Eh heyyyy toro! Eh heyyy torito! Eh heyyyy!"

Chester recognized the familiar jerky motion of the bull's head. He sees him.

"Eh heyyy!"

Ojos Negro started his charge from thirty yards away. El Encanto, with both feet planted inside his bullfighter's cap, looked as unconcerned as a man reading a newspaper in his favorite cafe. As the bull came to him, he changed the animal's direction from his front to his back by swinging the muleta behind him. After four of these statuesque passes, many of the people were calling out in delirium. The danger that El Encanto was running was evident in everyone in the arena. If the bull decided not to follow the movement of the cloth from front to back, he would drive straight into El Encanto.

After two more of these passes, he shuffled his feet around and did four pases de la muerta, the pass that allows the bull to pass under the fighter's armpit. Many could remember Jesus Gonzales being gored through the chin doing the pase de la muerta, the bull hooked upward in the middle of the pass. El Encanto fixed the bull in place with a cleverly designed signature movement and faded back a few yards to give the animal a chance to rest. The aficion applauded wildly.

He caught the bull's attention after a few beats and started a second series of interwoven passes. The opening pass was the Arrucina, the dangerous pass invented by Carlos Arruza, the fighter holding the muleta around behind his back, offering the bull the barest edge of the muleta as a lure. Most matadors would have been satisfied to do one. El Encanto did four, and then the left handed natural with the help of the sword, while smiling up at the audience.

Many purists were appalled when Manolete first performed his looking-at-the-public act. Chester folded his arms on the top of the barrera, placed his chin in the crook of his arm and studied the scene in front of him. El Encanto seemed to be doing a dance with the bull, wrapping him around and around in slow motion. The critics, even the people who hated him were screaming "Ôle, òle, òle, òle," almost a continuous chant.

And finally, at the logical conclusion to a dangerously beautiful faena, he dropped the bull with one clean thrust, crossing straight over the right horn. The sword disappeared into the bull's body as though it were being swallowed. The ritual had been performed, the sacrifice made, the monster was once again appeased.

El Encanto and his cuadrilla were given a triumphant parade around the bullring.

"Chester, my friend, come. They want to adore us." Chester, his trembling knees under better control now, joined the others for the parade. The aficion rained flowers, hats,

74

wineskins filled with wine. They took great pleasure in seeing the matador hold the bota up and shoot a jet stream of wine down his throat.

"Chester, here, have some wine." By the time the parade was over Chester and El Encanto were semi-tipsy. El Encanto was forced to go to the center of the ring, to The Middle of the World, at the conclusion of the parade.

"You are the greatest matador in history!" they shouted. "Long live El Encanto," they shouted.

"You are a master of the faena!" they shouted.

El Encanto acknowledged the frenzy, holding up the hooves and the tail that he had been awarded, the response to a sea of white handkerchief waving in the arena.

"You are the best of the best!" they shouted.

"And you are all a bunch of fucking assholes," he shouted back, his voice lost in the din, a smile on his handsome face. In the limo taking them back to the after-the-bullfight party, Ernesto Suares poured cognac and philosophized about the fight.

"You see how it is, my friend, one moment they hate you and the next moment they love you."

Chester, feeling a little cocky after thinking about the part he had played in the dripping drama, decided to probe. "But look, Ernesto, let's face it, the crowd had a legitimate gripe about the way you dealt with your first bull. I mean, let's face it, man, that was a fantastic animal and you messed around with it." Chester felt, for a moment, that he had overstepped the boundaries of polite conversation. El Encanto, unruffled, sipped his cognac before answering.

"Yes, you are correct, it was a fantastic bull but I did not mess around with it. I survived it." Tito held his glass over for a refill, a silly look of adoration glowing on his face. "If I had allowed the unrealistic sense of ego to intrude on my consciousness, I would not be sitting here, drinking this

75

excellent cognac with you, my friend. I would be on an operating table, my balls or my ass punctured by that fantastic animal's horns.''

"But how do you know that?'' Chester was feeling a little drunk and exasperated. "How do you know you could not have had an incredible fight with that bull?''

El Encanto held up his glass in a silent toast to the crowd milling around the limo. They had traveled a hundred yards in fifteen minutes. They chanted, "EL-EN-CAN-TO! EL-EN-CAN-TO! EL-EN-CAN-TO!''

Ernesto turned back to Chester's question, an uncharacteristically solemn expression darkening his features. "Chester, my friend, I am now twenty-eight-and-a-half years old. I have been in this life for nineteen years. I have seven great wounds from the bulls, one of them missed the hole of my ass by a half an inch.''

Chester flinched involuntarily, the sphincter muscles in his rectum tightened up.

"I have suffered many greater wounds outside the bullring but those are not important. We are speaking only of the corrida. I have experienced the emotion of feeling love for a wild, untamable creature that I had to kill in order to gain status in the society I live in. And I have also felt hate for the beast.'' The limo finally broke to the fringes of the adoring crowd and onto the boulevard. "You know, when I was a boy, I used to sneak into the pastures, as we did that night outside Valencia.''

"I remember, I remember.''

"I used to stay in the pastures with the bulls all night. Sometimes, I would take my muleta and do a few passes with them. Other times I would just climb a tree or onto a big rock and just study them. The bull is very, very complex animal and you must study his mind, his, his...''

"Psychology?''

76

"Yes, if you are going to be successful fighting the bulls, you must know them as well as they know themselves." He paused to pour more cognac all around. The car was bubbling with good vibes. "In my first bull, El Rey, you saw a magnificent beast, beautiful horns, beautiful muscles, beautiful cojones." Manuel and Tito laughed at a private joke. "You saw a bull who looked like a designer bull, one tailor made for the fight. I saw a treacherous beast who wanted to kill me. His muscles give him the strength to believe that he is capable of killing anything. In the ancient days, they sometimes had contests between bulls and other animals; bears, tigers, even elephants and the bulls were often the winners. The bull you thought was so perfect was not perfect at all. I could see, from the opening charges, that he was much too smart to play with. He immediately knew the difference between the man and the cape."

"Maybe someone in a field, at night, had fought him, Matador," Manuel said, in a dry voice.

"Possible, possible. He was noble looking, but he did not have nobility in him. You understand what I'm saying, Chester, my friend?"

"I think so."

"The bulls, like men, are not always what they look like. For a man to be noble, or a bull to be noble, he must have a sense of dignity that can only come from having the right mother." Chester took a hard sip on his cognac. Was Ernesto playing games with him? Ernesto saw the skeptical look and overpowered it. "I am not joking with you, Chester, my friend. I am not. They say that the bull is given his strength and looks from his father and his heart and courage from his mother. How many men have had rotten fathers but were saved by mother's milk?" El Encanto answered his own rhetorical question. "Many have been saved, many."

"Okay, I understand what you're saying, but what's

mother's milk got to do with this bull you're talkin' about?''

"The bull, as beautiful as he was, did not have nobility. He was neurotic, mixed up. He hooked erratically with both horns, his movements were not smooth. I could see that I was going to have a problem killing him, because he was concentrating so hard on killing me.

"You know, Chester, my friend, from seeing many fights, that the most important thing is the kill. That is what it comes to. And it is very difficult to go in over the horn of an animal who is hooking this horn at your thigh, your stomach, your chest, your head. If I had had a pistola, I would have shot that motherfucker.''

Chester laughed with the other men, spilling a little of his drink. "Awright, I get the point. He was a mean spirited beastie.''

"Yes.''

"And you survived.''

"Yes.''

"What was the difference between him and that ugly creature that followed him?''

"Ahh hah! He was ugly, to be sure, Chester, my friend, but he had a good heart and he charged, as we say, like a nun. In a straight line, as though he were on a railway track. With such an animal, one can do almost anything.

"When I was much younger and crazier, I once made a few passes with such a bull while I was blindfolded.'' So it was true. Señora Bou-Gomez had told the truth. She saw it. "Do you think I would have allowed you to go in the ring with that first crazy bull?''

"I'm glad you didn't even think of it.''

"I did the right thing. I killed the first beast before he killed me and I have a great demonstration with the second bull. You agree, Chester, my friend?''

Chester held up his glass in a toast. "Yes, I agree.''

He was impressed by the strange logic of El Encanto's life but he had had enough of it. The day after the fight, he pulled Ernesto Suares off to one side and explained that he had to leave, he had to return to his own lifestyle.

"But Chester, my friend, you should stay with me. I'm fighting in Barcelona this weekend."

"Ernesto, my friend, I've had enough. I'm tired of the traveling, the crowds, all of it." He felt that he shouldn't have been so vehement, but it was the truth.

"Yes, Chester, my friend, I understand. I too feel the same way. That is why I'm going to retire at the end of this season."

"What'll you do if you don't fight the bulls?"

"I will go with this rich American blonde to her home in California, eat a lot, get fat, drink a lot, find different ways to cum, be miserable."

They embraced and held onto each other for a long, soulful moment. "Suerte to you, Chester, my friend, remember . . . a man must do what Destiny has decided for him to do, until his dying day, because there is no telling what is going to kill him."

Chapter 9

He stood in the aisle of the train, watching the sun pop up over the Spanish countryside, lost in thought. His thought patterns swirled in an irregular circle, from the carefree days of his youth in Mississippi, despite the horrors of American Apartheid, to his years with Josie, to the endless days and nights of prison life. He was always thinking of titles for a book about his fifteen year stint in the joint: "Scars and Bars," "Incarcerated," "Jailhouse Humor." They stayed with him for fifty miles. I wonder if anybody on the outside has ever given any thought to the kinds of jokes people tell each other in the pen? Who would be interested in it?

Wonder what the University of Chicago quartet is doing? Suzy, Bert, Marvin and what's-his-name? Wonder where the incredible diva Ife Ebuni is stirring up trouble? Have to remember to drop the Palermos a few lines. Idea, notions, things to do made him feel slightly anxious. Gotta stop drinking so much espresso. He had left the Mediterranean southeast, Alicante, in the spring and now it was almost August. He felt like a stranger returning home. Francisco Zurriaga met him with an offer of cafe espresso and cognac.

"Chester, you are appearing thinner, more serious."

"I agree. Traveling with El Encanto can make you skinny and very serious." Señora Bou-Gomez had cleaned his room, hung a picture of a charging bull over his bed. "I thought you might like to have a reminder of your time with the great El Encanto." And broke out a bottle of her finest horse piss. "Now then, tell me how it was."

He spent the first week back in town walking up and down familiar streets, enjoying the sights, sounds and smells of the small Spanish city.

"Ahhh, Señor Manresa, what're we having in the Cafe El Canario today?"

"The touristas, fried hot dogs and chili sauce. For you paella a la Alicante."

Ana, his former ladyfriend, blindsided him in the fleamarket. "Cheester, I didn't know you was back. You had not contact me."

"Ana, it's over, don't you remember? You told me that you never wanted to see me again. And besides, your husband..."

"My husband, he is in manubers in Asturias. He will no be here until October." He made an oblique escape, feeling too jaded and wise, at fifty-one years old, to run the risk (again) of trying to deal with a promiscuous woman with a jealous husband. "Ana, look I have an appointment. Let's get together for a glass of wine sometime, okay? Bueno?" He couldn't resist turning to take a last look at the behind that caused him to break a long standing rule: Don't fuck other men's wives.

Chapter 10

Midnight. He sat in front of his open window, looking out onto the backyard of Alicante, a notebook and a stack of miscellaneous notes on the right side of his desk, a bottle of Jerez de la Frontera and a glass on the left. From somewhere beyond the irregular, jagged pattern of lights, he could hear a cacophony of sounds: a mother loudly explaining something to her children, a family dinner, a dog howling, a donkey braying, the lamenting music of North Africa throbbing from a shortwave receiver.

He had been stunned to hear so much African music being played. No one seemed interested in dancing to it, but they played it. "Africa, sí, she is right over dere. We like."

He sipped a glass of wine, alternately staring out of the window and staring at his pile of notes. How in the hell should I start on this? Should I use El Encanto's real name? Should I tell the truth about his lifestyle, the way I think he thinks? He shuffled through his notes, making notes within

82

the notes, rewriting the outline he had rewritten twice, doodling, pausing for another glass of wine. And another.

Finally, after three evenings of the same routine, he realized he was putting off the inevitable. "It was not five o'clock in the afternoon, as the story is traditionally told, but three a.m., on a moonlit night, somewhere in a pasture outside the city of Valencia." There, I've taken the first step...

He sat in front of his window every evening, trying to screw up the courage to write another paragraph, another page. As his partner, "Ol' Patcheye" used to say, "It's a little like trying to shit bricks."

Señora Sarafina Sanches Bou-Gomez, a pathological gossip (he had discovered), asked him one afternoon, "What is it that keeps you awake so late?"

"I am writing a book about the bullfight, Señora. Don't you remember? That's the reason why I traveled for three months with El Encanto.."

"Ahhhh, siiii!"

Two days later, Señor Manresad (Cafe El Canario) asked him, "How is the book about the bulls coming along?"

The manager of the bodega, where he purchased his Jeres de la Frontera, had advice. "Please, Señor, don't write about the bulls. It makes us seem like such a bloodthirsty people."

Francisco Zurriaga, the taxi driver, was puff-up about having introduced El Encanto's name to him. "Wheel I have a big place in the book?"

He soft pedaled the gossip and denied the truth until the commotion died down. From that point he became an honorary citizen of the city. An inhabitant of his particular section of town. A man who like the look of a woman's body, but was not disrespectful, a man who could drink wine with the men and not get disgracefully drunk. And he was an African-American writer. He insisted that they refer to him

83

as an African-American. And he could legitimately claim to be a working writer after a query letter to *La Izquierda*, the left-leaning newspaper in Madrid, earned him a commission to do twenty articles on the life of an African-American writer in Spain.

He smiled often at the irony of being able to write something, anything, about being an African-American, a subject that had never/or ever was, a particularly popular topic in America. He was being paid twenty-five dollars (3,100 pesetas) per article. It was money that allowed him to deal with his daily expenses and keep away from his main pile. "Shit, if this keeps up, I might wind up living over here."

El Encanto sent him one-hundred dollars (12,400 pesetas) in a plain brown envelope. "I'm on the road to Salamanca and, as you may have heard or read by now, my last three fights have been total tragedies. I hope the bulls in Salamanca have more respect for my art.

"This money is payment for your work with the banderillas in Pamplona. How goes the book? Ciao, Ernesto."

Same old El Encanto, full of life.

The articles seemed to unlock a lot of memories and thoughts about the weeks he had spent with El Encanto and the bull that his landlady had hung above his bed caused him to have nightmares. He took it down and stabbed it with his ballpoint. The twice re-written outlines, the stack of notes and the pages of the notebook were gradually being transformed into a book. He tried to discipline himself into writing ten pages an evening and failed. He failed to do five pages three evenings in a row and on the fourth evening, he wrote fifteen pages. "El Encanto is right, a man must do what Destiny has decided for him to do, until his dying day, because there is no telling what is going to kill him."

He grew a salt and pepper beard, feeling the spirit of

Chester Himes on him, strolled the beach at evening time and wrote throughout the summer. He was shocked to discover that he had completed the first draft of the novel after three months of complete dedication.

Wowwww...

He waded back through the work, straightening out kinks, making obscure comments clearer, re-writing whole chapters. The second re-write gave birth to a third and a fourth, 'til he was reasonably satisfied with it.

Well, what the fuck, it's the best I can do. He spent a Friday and a Saturday night at the Club Tropical, suddenly aware that he had been living a celibate, unperfumed life. As much as he loved women, he found himself almost unable to be sociable, to flirt with them, in the midst of a heavy writing schedule. It was almost as though the emotions he felt for women were like the emotions that he felt for writing. "Better be careful, Chester, my friend. Your pen might wind up becoming your pee-pee."

Twenty-six query letters later, a small publishing house in Darien, Connecticut, decided that they would take a look at the "Enchanted Arena." He had been explicit in his query letter about the subject matter of his book. I hope these assholes don't think that I'm sending them a boxing book or something about mud wrestling.

The articles, meanwhile, seemed to pour out of him. "We have to clearly understand what a literary bantustan is for the African-American writer in America. It means that his 'passbook' makes him ineligible to write movie reviews (even about so-called black movies), restaurant reviews (only whites eat and write about ethnic cuisines), political essays, commentary on the nuclear state of the world, book reviews about non-African-American subjects (only whites can write about writing), art criticism, cultural expressions of any kind (even African-American classical musical critiques are white-written). In other words, the African-American writer can only find space in the dominant culture's books, magazines, newspapers, etc., if he or she is willing to weave a note of subtle subservience into what is written. This note of subservience has several tones. As of this moment, to take an example, a number of books by African-American females are being published by the white male-dominated publishing industry in the United States. The note of subservience, or one of the tones that subservience by most of these African-American female writers, is that they should design an African-American man as a main character, who is either a brute, a super-masculine menial, an inept scuffer or a sex-crazed maniac. Or all of the above.

"Of course, not all African-American female writers buy into this subservience and they are not published as regularly. The same subservience holds true for the male side of the coin. If an African-American male writer can bring himself to declassify the women of his family, of his race, into a subspecies called 'bitch', the publishing industry (the same white guys) has use for him. There are those who would deny that there is a common thread running through most of the books that are being commonly published by the industry, that the thread reinforces negative behavior between African-American men and women.

"An objective analysis of any of the current books would be the greatest testimony this writer can offer to counter the denial."

Three months later, Franklin House Publishing Company of Darien, Connecticut, sent him a contract and an invitation to submit other works.

Fifteen articles later, *La Izequiera* commissioned him to do another series of articles. The following Sunday, decked out in a pin-striped three piece suit and a bow tie, almost caricaturing the "successful" author, he bent to pick up a copy of his favorite paper, turned to the sports section to discover a flattering photograph of Ernesto Suares, El Encanto. "El Encanto, a well known matadore who has experienced various levels of success in his art, was found gored to death, in a pasture on the ranch of Don Miquel de Uva. It appears that the matador was attacked by several bulls at one time, at some hour between twelve midnight and six a.m. He had announced his impending retirement (his third) at the end of the current season. Next of kin have been notified."

Chester tucked the paper under his arm and marched into his favorite bar.

"I'll have two cognacs, please."

"Two cognacs, señor?"

"One for me, and one for him."

He sat at the bar, sipping two cognacs at a time, staring at El Encanto's picture, remembering . . . "A man must do what Destiny has decided for him to do, until his dying day, because there is no telling what is going to kill him."

Chapter 11

"The Enchanted Arena" was a critical success. He didn't make millions on the first printing but it put his name on a few thousand minds. "The Survival Tango" was also well-received. He could measure the level of popularity by closely monitoring the number of undiscovered relatives who suddenly surfaced. "Uhhh, you don't know me, but I'm your third cousin on your mother's side."

The years of prison life had taught him the art of living simply, so he didn't feel the need to move into more expensive surroundings, which flattered Señora Sarafina Sanchez Bou-Gomez. "When I saw your book, I thought, he will move into el centro, into the big hotel, buy the big car, become a Biggie."

He laughed at her comments and continued having an occasional horse piss sipping session with her. She was an invaluable source of Spanish history and, on occasion, world history. "You must remember, the state of things in Europe, in 1937 were very very difficult. The conditions were ripe for a dictator, or a Hitler. Or a Franco. And a Mussolini. Sometimes, people do not remember these things. And the conditions from that time are responsible for the conditions of these times."

Whenever the need arose, he would rent a room in one of the fancier hotels and seduce a woman. His favorite seductees were "liberated" North African women. They came across the Mediterranean, from Tunisia, Libya, Algeria, Morocco, Egypt. They were doctors, lawyers, financial experts, writers, actresses, politicians, musicians, people on the move, and they came to Spain, as an African outpost in Europe, to chill out, have a drink, take a break from the residual chauvinism in their homelands.

"You cannot possibly know what it means to be a woman, with a brain, running a bank in Egypt." The woman, the director of a Barclay's branch in Cairo, sprawled beside him in the oversized bed, sipping a Bloody Mary breakfast.

"But wait a minute, you're the director of a bank, the person in charge..."

"But I am also a woman, and I have been asked to make tea, to serve coffee. I have been insulted by men who knew only how to herd camels and beat their wives. When I was a girl, because I was a member of the elite, the old-fashioned elite, I was circumcised..."

"You were what?"

"They performed a female circumcision on me."

Life in Alicante was infinitely interesting and he relished, savored it. The place was small enough for people to become familiar strangers, but only the totally uncouth took it upon themselves to become nuisances.

"The Enchanted Arena" was translated into Spanish and he held his breath for a couple of weeks, afraid to find out what the Alicante intelligentsia, the literary people, thought of it. Señora Bou-Gomez, the collector of gossip, brought him the majority opinion. "Señor, your bullfight story is approved of by the people."

The challenge had been met. He had learned a great deal about the arena in which the writer fought the readers, from El Encanto. "You must remember, Chester, my friend, most people have no idea of who they really are or what they really want. They are not like us, killers of bulls or writers of words. They are simply people, wandering around, eating, drinking, trying to figure out what they should be. Sabes?"

He sat in front of his Alicante window, listening to the stray strands of Flamenco that reached him, the sudden yell or scream, the loud talk of the arguing people. It was all beginning to sound too familiar, but at the same time, it continued to be strange. He felt the need to take a break, go to another rhythm, experience a different type of people. He stirred the idea of taking a trip to Scandinavia around in his brain for a week. He felt a vague urge to write a book on the origins of white racism, but gave up after a week of crisscrossing thoughts had placed too many obstacles in his way.

"Our Music" reached into his third dream and forced him to start making notes for a new book. "Our Music", a musical tribute in prose to Malcolm X, Martin Luther King, Jr., and Marcus Garvey, the triple MMM's of the African-American world. One evening, he sat in front of his Alicante window, listening to a Gypsy lament that was so blue that he cried for ten minutes, not even bothering to try to trace the source of his tears. Feels like I need to take my ass on back over there, back to Amerikkka. Señora Sarafina Sanchez Bou-Gomez assured him that his room would be secure.

"Ahhh, my friend, you have no need to concern yourself. There will always be a place in my house for you."

The commissioned articles for *La Izquierda* had become

a bi-weekly column. He could send pieces in about whatever struck his fancy and be paid for them. One of the editors of the paper referred to him as 'the black Andy Rooney' of journalism. He knew that the remark was meant to be complimentary, but he wasn't flattered. The next piece he sent in was dedicated to an expose of the narrowness of ethnocentric thinking. Why should a handsome African-American movie actor be referred to as a black Clark Gable, or a black Robert Redford. Or an African-American mathematical genius called the black Albert Einstein. Chester L. Simmons was not called the black Andy Rooney again. "Yeahhh, it's time to go on back over there and see what them fools is doin'."

A strong urge pulled him toward Africa, right across the Mediterranean, but he didn't want to take the two week tour, or the two month tour. He wanted to sink his feelings into the continent and hang in for a few years, to unravel some things. He felt no need to trip to Africa in order to find out if that's where he came from, he already knew that. He felt no need for daishikis, or other superficial ornaments to demonstrate his loyalty to the Motherland. He was always there in his soul, and he knew that, too. No, Africa wasn't going anywhere. It would be there, waiting for him whenever he got ready for it.

This is a different urge. He was tired of struggling with a different language, a different mind-set, different sets of attitudes. He felt the need for something familiar, really familiar. "Shit, I want some corn bread n' greens."

It took him too full weeks to stroll around town, to say "Adios" to all of the people he had become friendly with, the people who had offered him friendship and guidance from the beginning.

"Si, is very important to return, to re-fill the mind." Francisco Zurriage had no problem understanding his motivation for returning. There were others, more politically motivated than emotional, who didn't want to understand.

"Why go back to all that? You do realize that fascism, and of course, racism is re-surfacing. Why return to that?"

"Auuu c'mon, José, racism and fascism is alive and well in Spain, and always has been. Look at Mexico, wherever the Spanish did their number in South America and elsewhere."

"There is some truth to what you say. But I must remind you that we Spaniards have only been racist abroad and never at home. Our Moorish background did a great deal, I suspect, to discourage outright racist behavior."

He was in mid-ocean when he suddenly realized that his return to the United States meant returning to a low point on the pole. Maybe Papa Palermo will give me my old job back. Let me wait on a few tables.

He felt like a new man, powerful, a Somebody. He had left America as a servant and returned as an author, a Somebody . . .

God, I wonder where that Ebuni woman is. I wonder if she was a real person? Of course, she was real. She was the one who pulled my ass outta here.

He rented a car and decided to tour the town for a few hours, to see how much had changed and how much had remained the same. He started at the beach. Redondo Beach at midday was like a fairy land to him. Alicante, on the beach, the fishermen pull in the fish for the town's dinner. Here, the fishermen pull in the tourists. Oh, well . . .

What next? From the beach to the so-called inner city. He could never figure out why the adjectives 'inner-city' were used to describe Watts. Somehow, it seemed to him an area that spread out over so many miles could hardly be described as an 'inner city'. But he clearly understood the code, 'inner city' meant the place where the African-American lived.

Barrio meant where the Mexicans and other people from South America lived. The areas where white people were the majority were simply called residential areas.

The police stopped him driving west on 103rd Street. "Step away from your vehicle and keep your hands in sight."

He studied the two white men as they checked his license, probed for weaknesses in his psychological make-up. "When did you do your last bit?"

"Beg your pardon?"

"Don't try to play funny man with us, Chester. When and where did you do your last bit?"

Chester? Interesting. They check my driver's license and suddenly they can get to know me so well, I'm Chester. His understanding of the police mentality, after a fifteen-year stint with that kind of mindset, offered him a rare insight. There, two keepers of the colony called Watts (Bantustan) wanted to shoot him and they needed only a hair trigger motivation to do it. He played them away from their anxiety, mistrust and urges to kill by allowing a West African lilt to seep into his voice. Even racist policemen gave more consideration to imports.

"Gentlemen, I'm out of my element. I was looking for the Watt's Towers and I seem to be lost. Perhaps you could give me some direction." The policemen exchanged coded signals. "Where you from, Chester?" one of them asked him, his hand still perched on the handle of his pistol.

"I'm originally from Accra, Ghana, West Africa." Give 'em the full number so that they won't be confused. West Africa, not the west side.

"What're you doing here?"

"I'm in the import-export business." Once again, they exchanged coded looks.

"That's not what I'm asking you, Chester. I'm asking what your business is in this area?"

93

He felt compelled to give into the urge to say, that's none of your fuckin' business! but decided, rationally, to cool it.

"As I said, officer, I'm looking for the Watts Towers. I've been told that it's a fantastic structure and..."

The cop cut him off by abruptly handing his license back. "That bunch o' junk you want to see is back the other way. I'd be careful trippin' around on this turf, Chester, the gangs are kinda dangerous, you know?"

Chester flashed his all encompassing bullshit smile and slowly got back into his car. Rotten motherfuckers. He sat in the car for a few moments, collecting himself. "Why in the fuck did I come back to this jive ass place?" He looked out at the small herd of teenaged boys drifting past him. A couple of them looked into the car at him, as though he were a potential prospect for a robbery. He decided to leave the neighborhood. Why take chances?

Chapter 12

The Palermos greeted him like a prodigal soon. In the space between the shrimp marinara, the fettucine Alfredo, Chianti ("Straight from fuckin' Italy, man"), dessert, coffee and cognac, he was forced to explain why he hadn't written more often. "I really can't offer any excuses, folks. All I can say is that you're like a family to me and I should've made a greater effort to keep in touch."

They stared at his name on the covers of "The Enchanted Arena" and "The Survival Tango" and finally touched the books as though they were sacred.

"Buddha, these are yours, you wrote 'em?"

"I did, indeed."

He decided to skip 'Marbene', in the interest of keeping emotional confusion to a minimum. The Mission was still there, but the Reverend Whitbred was gone, long gone. The new man in charge delicately explained, "Well, if you knew the Reverend as well as you say you do, then you are aware that he had a few personal problems."

"Don't we all?"

"I suppose so, Mr...?"

"Chester Simmons."

"You're correct, Mr. Simmons, but we're not all alcoholics." He took the news like a dead weight. He really didn't feel totally surprised. After all, anybody could be anything in today's world.

He rented a room in one of the transient hotels in Hollywood ("by the day, week or month"), turning away from Palermo Jr.'s offer to become a roommate again. ("It wouldn't be a problem, Buddha, believe me"), and prowled the Los Angeles basin for a week, casually searching for a reason to remain on the West Coast. The magic was gone. The sense of the exotic, the challenge of being in a new environment was dead. He was no longer excited by the spaces that made a trip to the supermarket a safari, or the startling diversity of the people. Of the beauty of the women. He wandered around for another week, going for a stroll on the beach, to Griffith Park, to a few jazz houses, felling more and more dissatisfied.

The local soulfood restaurant (Broadway and Slauson Avenues) had supplied him with all the cornbread and greens he'd ever need for days. But there was something else troubling him, something he had a problem pinning down.

"This fuckin' place is too big..."

The thought closed in on him as he drove from a journey to Long Beach ("see the Queen Mary") back to his hotel. "This fuckin' place is too big...I feel like I'm on a treadmill, riding hundreds of miles between supermarket aisles." He had made an effort to drive from Vermont Avenue and Sunset Boulevard to wherever Vermont came to an end and surrendered to distractions, after he passed Manchester and discovered that there was still more Vermont to travel.

"Nawww, this ain't the scene for me. I need to be somewhere where I can get to know people, get to know the scene, figure out what the deal is."

Sitting up in bed writing, the third week in town, the hot childhood memory of Mississippi flashed through his mind. "The South, that's where I need to be, back where things are Real. But I can't go back to Mississippi. Mississippi was filled with too many bittersweet memories. Mississippi was a beautiful Indian word chock full of lynched Black bodies, raped Black women, cotton fields full of whipped souls. No, no Mississippi for Buddha. They're always talking about Atlanta. Maybe I'll take that route. One thing is certain, Georgia ain't Mississippi."

He toyed with the idea of trying to do a Truman Capote, "In Cold Blood", on Wayne Williams, the young black man who had been tried and convicted of the murder of the children slaughtered in Atlanta. He remembered conversations he had had with his fellow convicts during the heat of the Williams trial. The consensus was that the man was being framed to take the heat off of the guilty party or parties. Ol' Patcheye, one of the most astute thinkers he'd ever met, offered a three parts lecture. "Number one, we know, based on all the circumstantial evidence they've exposed us to, that the dude is definitely not guilty." And that's gall they've thrown at us, circumstantial evidence.

"Number two, the fact that they're in such a hurry to convict this dude of all these murders, despite the fact that they've only offered circumstantial evidence or one of the murders is proof positive, in my eyes, uhhh, in my eye, hah, hah, hah, hah...that he's a scapegoat.

"Number three, we know that there has to be white involvement in the deal somewhere, simply because they've made such an overwhelming effort to make us believe there ain't no white folks involved.

"I've put all the stuff that I've learned over a lifetime of being a crook in the United States, the Caribbean and elsewhere together, and I've come up with two theories.

"A: one of the experimental labs got caught with its drawers down, and had to deflect public opinion right quick. B: one of those regulation white hate groups, the Klan or the Aryan Brotherhood, or the U.S. Nazis, or what have you, simply went crazy for a while and since the U.S. government is basically an extension of one of those groups, they simply found someone to sacrifice."

Chester decided to leave the Wayne Williams case alone. "I just don't have the resources to get into it." He knew he'd need legal consultants, a research staff, a support group, if he really wanted to do an A-1 job. "Nawww, I can't do it. Beyond everything else, they'd be tryin' to snare my ass in a web in a minute, an ex-con, a murderer."

But the die was cast for him to trip South. It was as though the trip to Europe with Ife Ebuni and living in Spain for a while had unlocked an urge to travel. He took one last circle around the basin, from the ocean to the mountains, before boarding a train to Atlanta.

Chapter 13

The days and nights became dawns and sunsets and, from time to time, seemed to merge. He tilted himself into the rest position and allowed his consciousness to become a part of the trains rhythms. He fasted for two days.

"Why eat? I'm not using any energy. I'm just sitting here."

In the middle of the night or just before dawn he had fiercely sexual dreams, lured into position by the insistent rhythm of the train. He licked the giant scoop of ice cream that was sculpted like a woman's cunt. The lips on each side of the clitoris glowed a deep umber and the melting cream gave off the aroma of fully bloomed roses. His tongue fished around inside the gentle folds of the cunt, the tip of it filled with microscopic dick heads, each of them filled with tiny, perfectly formed tongues. He cupped his erection under the blanket and smiled. Mmmmmmm...

The miles of America oozed past him in the dark, spilling

Twilight Zone images through the darkened window. He wrote stories about twinkling lights in the distance, novelettes about thoughts that were triggered by subliminal ideas. Marcus Garvey mounted his subconscious for a hundred miles, parading thousands of African-Americans through the Harlems of the mind, reminding him of a past that most Black people in America knew little about. Garvey's plumed admiral's hat and his black moon face was replaced by the intensity of Malcolm X's eyes and the raised vein that pulsed down the center of his intelligent forehead as he spoke the truth about and to the former slave owners. And to the descendents of the former slaves. Stray sentences from Malcolm X's speeches sliced through his consciousness like a razor. "We must look out for us. You will never get justice and freedom from the white man in America. An eye for an eye and a tooth for a tooth, a head for a head and a death for a death."

Chapter 14

Martin Luther King, Jr.'s image superimposed on Malcolm X's face at dawn. He tried to concentrate on other ideas, other images, hoping to blot out the persistence of Martin Luther King, Jr.'s message of "love the enemy."

I don't wanna hear no shit like that. I don't wanna hear no shit like that...

"Uhhh, pardon me, sir, are you all right?"

He stared up at the pale face and into the pale grey eyes of the Amtrack stewardess. "Uhh, yes, I was just having a little dream fight with myself." She flashed an Amtrack-trained smile in his general direction and faded away.

The grandeur of the continent overwhelmed him. Damn, this is a big fuckin' country. The images of magnificent Indian cultures and the ways they had been degraded caused him to grit his teeth. The solemn reddish faces that moved through the aisle as they passed through New Mexico almost caused him to cry. Apaches in Arizona, Hopis, Navajos in

New Mexico, the Kiowa, Wichitas, Arapahoe, Cheyennes, Chickachono; the cross section of Indian tribes that he had read about in the prison library, seemed to stare into his window from behind the prairies, the hills, the trees, the horizon. I must be hallucinating.

He allowed himself to be suckered into conversations just to break the monotony that was so abstractly interesting to him.

"Names Cramshank, Morgan. What's yours?"

"Simmons, Chester, Louis."

"Traveling far?"

"All the way to Georgia."

"That's far."

He had found out how really dull people could be by traveling non-luxury (bus/train). Except for four exceptions, the people who found a conversation with him irresistible, were addicted to a level of dialogue that automatically eliminated any serious discussion about 1) racism, 2) politics, 3) art, 4) music of any kind, 5) dance, 6) literature of any kind, 7) the PLO, 8) South Africa, 9) African-American history, 10) Euro-American history. In effect, any serious subject.

He made a sharp contrast between this American habit of reflecting a game show mentality and the conversations he had had on European trains and busses. Honest peasants in Spain wanted to know what effect the new president was having on the American psyche. Scandinavian teenagers were concerned about the effect of American guilt complexes on their film industry. "We find it difficult to understand the American attitude about sex."

He was beginning to feel that he was dead. Or in a dream state that was forever changing scenery. The half hour layover in Jackson, Mississippi was his tip-off that he was not dead. Or in a dream state.

It was midspring and beyond the stench of train station smoke, he could smell vague hints of magnolia, wisteria and fresh manure. He strolled out of the station and stood on a nearby corner for a few minutes. I wonder which way Chitlin Switch is from here? I wonder how far it is from here? The sudden flood of childhood memories almost caused him to miss his departure. "Wotch yo' step there, Mister!"

The pleasant tone of voice and the twinkle in the white conductor's eyes surprised him. He settled back into his seat, remembering. They used to call me nigger so often, I thought that was part of my name, Nigger Chester. "Didn't you hear what I said?" the conductor said.

Mississippi, the one room school with the Lil' Black Sambo textbooks and the middle-aged Negro woman who was pulling off the supreme trick of pleasing the four man county schoolboard (all white) and convincing the Black children in her room that they were as good as anybody else.

"Mornin' Sally, how're the little niggers doin' today?"

"O, they're doin' just fine, Mr. Coldstraw, just fine. Children, say good mornin' to Mr. Coldstraw."

"Mornin' Mr. Coldstraw!"

Memories. Mr. Coldstraw, of the County School Board, strolling down the aisles, patting the students on the head like puppies and just before leaving the classroom, patting Mrs. Sally Rivers on the behind as though she were one of his mules.

Memories. Mornings that were glazed by sunshine, humid, filled with ten year-old-boy-things to do, the lazy river three miles down the road to catch perch from, the cotton fields on both sides of the road, the frothy bulbs billowing up from the horizon, friends.

Lodean Preston. He closed his eyes and savored the name and the sweetness of all it represented. Lodean Preston, my first girlfriend. Lodean Preston. If this were a movie now,

I'd be doing a flashback, looking out on these fields. Maybe a cloud or something would drift in from somewhere and I'd be back there, ten years old again. Despite his attempt to push the thought of a flashback away by being satirical, the sight of the fields whizzing past did take him back. Lodean Preston, three big coils of braided hair, skin as black and shiny as an eggplant, a precocious fourteen year set of breasts and buttocks mounted or her ten year old frame. They had experience pure pleasure with each other and suffered no bad consequences, physically or morally.

"Lodean, I don't think we oughta be doin' this, I swear I don't."

"Why not, you luv me, don'tcha?"

"Uh huh."

"Well, this what people do when they luv each other."

"But, but. . ."

"But what?"

"What if you get big?"

"Chester, I can't get big."

"What?"

"I can't get big, 'cause I ain't had no period yet. Boys don't know nothin'."

They had spent a summer and a winter connected to each other; he couldn't think of a better word to describe their attachment to each other. Semi-rural children (Chitlin Switch had a population of 285), they had often watched mules, pigs, chickens, horses and occasionally, surreptitiously, people perform the sex act, but they had to find out how the physical act gave way to something else, something called love.

"Chester, I luv you so much."

"I luv you too, Lodean."

In the loft of a barn, over the course of the summer, Lodean Preston had taught him as much about love and lovemaking as he would ever know.

104

"Chester, pull it out for a minute. Let me look at it."

"Huh?"

"Lemme see what it look like."

"Can I look at yours, too?"

"If you wanna."

The stream of sunlight that caught the head of his penis seemed to make it glow. They sat in place, his pants and shorts draped around his ankles, her panties around her calves, her faded cotton dress pushed up over her lush young hips, staring at the glistening pearl of cum that oozed from the lips of his penis. She bent over and kissed the pearlike droplet from the tip. Forty years later, traveling through the state where it happened, he felt the warmth of her kiss again.

"You said I could look at you, too." She had laid back in the fragrant straw. He saw the movement in slow motion. He sprawled between her legs and stared at the glistening petals.

"What do it look like?" she had asked him.

He smiled at the memory, a cotton field worker waving at the train.

"It look like a . . . it look kinda like a . . . like a pretty flower, with petals and stuff." He kissed the little button glittering in the shaft of sunlight, the way she had kissed him. And felt a shiver come from all over her body. He did it again. And again. And each time she shivered more.

"Chester," she whispered as though she couldn't catch her breath, "Chester, lemme do that to you whilst you doin' that to me." God, if ol' man Preston had caught us up there he would've had a heart attack and then he would've killed both of us with his bare hands.

But they hadn't been caught, not then or at any other time. And, as suddenly as it had started, it ended. He remembered it as being one of the coldest winters they'd ever had. It was on a Monday and she hadn't come to school. She wasn't there on Tuesday and by Wednesday, he was feeling a little crazy. Who could he ask about her disappearance? He had made a studied effort to ignore her in school, in order to maintain his status among his peers. It would never do for June Bug, Percy Burton, Melvin Bates, Clifford Sawyer and the rest of the gang to get an inkling that his heart was cracking because Lodean Preston wasn't around.

He ran a mile out of the way to walk past the Preston place after school. It was deserted. He had never been so puzzled and disturbed in his whole life. Finally, unable to contain himself, he stood beside his mother, watching her make biscuits from scratch, and asked, "Momma, what happened to the Prestons? I went by...I passed by they place and ain't nobody there no mo'."

His mother had wiped the flour and dough onto her apron and hugged him as she told him, "Didn't nobody tell you, did they? Sam Preston got into trouble with the white folks and they had to get away."

"Got into trouble with the white folks?"

"Yes, honey. He got into trouble with the white folks. With that ol' nasty ol' man named Coldstraw. Now don't you go' round talkin' 'bout this, y'hear?"

"Yes'sum"

Forty years later the tears welled up in his eyes again. He had never seen her again.

Chapter 15

Atlanta was hot and popin', not a trace of *Gone with the Wind* in sight. People nodded to each other in that familiar Southern way, but there was a degree of hipness about the way it was done that was distinctly 'unsouthern'. He decided to rely on a familiar resource person, the city taxi driver, to find a place to stay, where to settle in. Halfway through Alabama, he had hit on the subject matter for his next novel. It was going to be a love story about a woman who had never experienced love. She would have children, grandchildren, an affair or two, but not love. She was going to be a real Southern belle, a black woman who had been convinced that all she had to do was maintain a certain kind of physical and emotional sanctity about herself and the Kingdom of Love was certain to come. She was not going to be Blanche DuBois, out of *A Streetcar Named Desire*. Nothing neurotic or weird about her. She was simply going to be a forty-year-old woman who hadn't found what we all need most.

"Taxi, mister?"

A very dark man with what seemed to be pinstriped marks on both cheeks signalled to him.

"Yes, brother, I need a taxi, a place to stay...somewhere real cheap and some information about the city." The man with the pinstriped cheeks loaded his suitcases in his cab without saying another word. Chester sat in the back seat, staring at the back of his head. And at his identifying photo and numbers in the passport-sized identity card posted on the back of the front seat.

Joseph Mensah.

"I detect an accent. You been here long?"

The taxi driver shot a straight look at Chester's face via the rear view mirror. "No."

Chester settled back. This was obviously not a friendly, loquacious tax driver. O well...

He could tell that the driver was wandering a bit to drive up the fare by the way he allowed himself to be caught by every red light they came to. Atlanta, obviously had been studying New York City closely and had decided to practice some of the Big Apple's worst habits. He decided not to press the driver for any information. Shit, ain't no telling what he'll give me. They came to a stop in front of a run down two story frame house. A dozen pairs of eyes lazered on him as he stepped out of the taxi.

"What's this?"

"Della Mae Jones' roomin' house. You say you want a cheap place to stay?"

Chester made a careful study of the situation. A dozen people, young, middle-aged, old, lounged around on the wrap around veranda of the rooming house. He had the sudden impression of being in Haiti, Jamaica or some other Third World country. The hump-thump of a ghetto blaster formed a heartbeat for the scene. The driver shifted from one foot to the other impatiently.

"Well?"

"You want to wait here to see if there's a vacancy?"

The cabbie frowned and pointed at a faded sign hanging from a corner of the veranda. "This is Della Mae Jones' roomin' house. There's always a vacancy."

He felt the urge to grab the brother's shoulders and shake him hard, to ask him, "What the fuck's wrong with you, man? What're you so pissed off about?" but he canceled the urge. Who knows? Maybe the guy's mother just died. Or his last fare maybe run out on him or something. He paid the inflated fare and gave the man a generous tip. As a reward, the driver's expression changed from mean to simply surly.

Della Mae Jones' Rooms. He felt like a laboratory specimen, struggling up to the veranda with two suitcases and an overnight bag. It was twilight and the springtime humidity had worn him down a bit. "Where can I find Miss Jones?" He directed his question to the person sitting on the veranda steps. The old man, almost a caricature of Uncle Remus, except for the heavy sour mash odor wreaking from his worn garments, pointed a negligent finger at a woman slumped in a rocking chair at the end of the veranda. Della Mae Jones could've been the African-American version of his Spanish landlady, Sarafina Sanchez Bou-Gomez. Her glazed eyes swept from Chester's head to his feet as he approached her, weaving through outstretched legs and slow moving conversation.

"Miss Jones?"

"That's me, honey."

"You got a room to rent?"

"If I didn't have one, I wouldn't have that sign up there sayin' that I did. C'mon, follow me." She struggled out of the rocking chair, a quivering mass of flesh in a gingham mu-mu. As she shuffled past the outstretched legs, she called out to different people in a surprisingly strong voice. "Mose, I thought I told you to rake up the yard an hour ago?"

Mose, the man sitting on the steps, looked up at her with a lazy grin on his face.

"May Lou, Coffee, Thimble, I don't want y'all out here smokin' none o' that dope on this porch whilst I'm inside, y'unnerstand?" The youthful trio she addressed nodded absently. Chester had half an urge to turn away, bolt down the steps and look for another place. "Maybe go to a Holiday Inn. But what the hell, I'm here now, may as well make the best of it."

She led him into a dingy front room that served as her office. "Sign yo' name here." She shoved a dog-eared registration book under his nose. He hesitated for a moment before signing.

"How long you plannin' to stay wid us?"

How long? "Uhhh, a couple weeks, maybe a month."

"Well, if you stayin' two weeks, you pay one week in advance, if you stayin' three weeks, that's two weeks in advance 'n so on."

He opted for two weeks. That'll give me a chance to look around, find a really decent place. Room 207 was on the second floor, overlooking the veranda.

"You're lucky, Mister Simmonszz!!!"

"You can call me Chester."

"And you can call me Della Mae. I was just gon' say, you're lucky. This is 'bout the choicest room in the place far as I'm concerned. We had a ol' man livin' up in here 'til last week."

"Oh, did he move?"

"Naw, he died, bless his soul, owing me three month's rent."

The room needed painting, it needed a new mattress on

the bed, it needed to have the cobwebs cleaned from the corners. She followed his eyes.

"Yeahhh, I know, it needs a little scrubbin' 'n fixin' up, but I can't git 'round to it, what with my heart condition and all this artha-ritis in my body."

He smiled a diplomatic smile and strolled over to look out of the window. He hadn't lived in an authentic Black ghetto in years. Bowen Avenue in Chicago, on the second floor with Josie. "It'll do just fine, Mrs. Jones, it'll do fine."

He sprawled on the swaybacked bed after she shuffled out, and fell into his first fully stretched out sleep in days. An hour later he was jolted from a deep, dreamless sleep by the sounds of a knock-down-drag-out fight in the next room. The yells and things being thrown didn't seem to attract much attention for awhile. Someone called out, "I wish you motherfuckers would give us a break up there!"

A half hour later, two sarcastic looking black cops put in an appearance. Chester peeked around the corner of his room door to see them pull a shirtless man out of the room, his wrists cuffed behind him. And then, fifteen minutes later, an ambulance came to carry out a blanket covered form on a stretcher. He stopped a man going into the hall toilet with a copy of the *Atlanta Constitution*. "What happened?"

"Awwww, he finally killed that bitch. I knew it was gon' happen sooner or later, the kinda shit she was doin'."

The Southern night allowed a relative peace to settle in, punctuated by pistol shots from nearby and a loud, drunken argument on the veranda below his window.

"Fuck with me and the groundhog'll be deliverin' yo' mail."

"Well, you know what they say, it take ass to git ass!"

"I ain't scared o' you, motherfucker!"

"You oughta be! If yo' momma raised you with any sense."

He felt semi-sluggish the next morning, tired from being awakened by ambulance and police sirens, passing cars with hump-thump sound systems, screams from the next house, what sounded like machine gun fire in the next block, miscellaneous noises that he couldn't identify. It was ten a.m., it was Friday the 13th, he was living in a rooming house in one of America's bantustans and it was eighty-five degrees and humid already. He wandered down onto the veranda, the common ground of the establishment. A few new faces (including his own) had been added to the core group. A couple quarts of beer was being circulated. Mrs. Jones called out to him from her chair. ''Hi' you doin' this monin', Chester?'' He saluted her with a weak wave and strolled down the street in search of some grits, sausage 'n biscuits.

After a week he had mastered a sleep pattern that made him feel almost rested. It depended on his ability to catnap every couple hours, before and after heavy bombardments. Damn, no wonder people who are forced to live in ghettos are always nervous, high strung, ready to fight. The fuckin' decibel level would make anyone up tight.

He was into ''Simone'' and, strangely, the violence, the noise, the uncertainty of the life around him, was helping him put a better story together. Byron Forbes, the editor at Franklin House, was enthusiastic about the upcoming new book and the books to come.

Dear Chester, he wrote, *you've opened our eyes onto the vistas of a world that, frankly, Franklin House didn't know about. We are opening up a section for material from the Black Experience and we look to you for guidance and 'ammunition'. Please feel free to contact me at any time. We're anxiously awaiting ''Simone''.*

I guarantee you she will find a home with Franklin House. Sincerely yours, . . .

He was on a roll and he knew it. All he had to do was write, write, write. His neighbors were curious about what he was doing and none more curious than Mrs. Della Mae Jones' daughter, May Lou. "Chester, anybody evah tell you you look like a fuckin' chinaman?"

"I'm afraid not, May Lou. Nobody ever told me that I looked like a fuckin' chinaman."

He had made several basic flirtational mistakes with May Lou. The first one, he admitted to himself, was to allow her to come into his room. The second one was to admire her body and face. May Lou was one of those peanut-colored African-American women who looked like a bunch of ripe grapes. He had the experience to know that the face with the Africoid-Native American cheekbones was going to slowly melt into blubber under the influence of her french-fries-fries-chili-cheese-dogs'n burgers-with-catsup diet. The breasts that spat at him through her see-through blouses were beginning to slop (at twenty-three), from lack of exercise; the wasp waister that shimmered down into a set of hips and thighs that would never win any Anglo-American beauty contests, thanks to the Orisha, but were a Black man's real gold mine, were beginning to accumulate. That was the only word he could think of that explained what was happening. She was *accumulating*.

"May Lou, you know something? You are really a fine, young sister, you know that?"

She had paused in her stroll through the hallway, a sister with the rhythm of a sister carrying a water jug on her head. She cocked her left thigh at him, stopped chewing her bubble gum for a split second and propped both hands on her beautifully designed hips. "You think so?"

"Yes, m'am, I definitely do."

His third flirtational mistake was to make love to her. It had become unavoidable, after three weeks of early summer

113

heat, wisteria, magnolia, pungent marijuana smoke, loud noises, pages and pages of "Simone." She had tapped on his door in the middle of a sensually slow-moving chapter.

"Whatchu dewin' in there?"

"I'm playin' with myself."

"Lemme see."

She had pushed into room 207, a gaudy polyester Japanese robe covering her bra and panties. "May Lou, what would your mother say, if she knew you were in my room? Do you know it's three a.m.?" She had laughed in his face, a full-fledged-deep-in-the-gut laugh.

"Chester, do you know that I am going on twenty-four years old and I got three babies?"

"I know all that, but you're still a daughter to your mother."

"My momma's asleep. Whatchu dewin' in here?" She sprawled on his bed and drifted into a deep bubble gum sleep as he read her the first chapter of "Simone". She woke up, smiling, as he fumbled with the catch to her bra. "These kind fasten in back."

He undressed her and, despite her sleepy protests, stood her up beside the sloppy bed, in the middle of Uzi machine gun fire, yelled curses from the house next door, the hump-thump box passing, the everlasting sound of sirens, that seemed to surround them as soon as the sun went down.

"Just stand there. Let me look at you."

"That all you gon' do?" She panted like a dog in heat when he gently fondled her gorgeous breasts and groaned so loudly when he caressed her clit with his tongue that he almost stopped. He wanted to make love, to enjoy her awhile, but decided to cum as quickly as possible because she was making such a loud drama of it all.

"Go 'head, daddy. Stick that dick to me, uhhh huhhh, that's it, daddy. Right there. This pussy is your'n.

114

Ooooowheeee, gimme that dick, daddy. Your dick is so good in my pussy! Ooooohhhh! Fuck me, daddy! Cum on in this pussy, daddy, its yours. Oooooohhwheeee! I'm cummmmmmmmmmmin', daddy. I'm cummmmmmmin' now! Awwwwhhheeee! Don't stop, please! Don't stop! Ohhh, my Gawd, this dick feel so good in my pussy! Ooooowhheeee! I'm commmmmmmin', daddy, I'm cummmmmin'!''

He had a slow-triple-ejaculation at the conclusion of her fifth orgasm and instinctively realized that he was going to have to flee the premises and never fuck May Lou again. She had, what his ol' convict partner, Ol' Patch, the one-eyed philosopher, once called, "intrinsically good pussy." Yes, she had intrinsically good pussy. And the next day, everyone in the rooming house knew that he had some of it, including her father, Mose, the Uncle Remus who habitually occupied the fourth step leading up to the veranda.

"We heard y'all last night,'' Mose whispered to him as he tried to make a nonchalant stroll down the steps.

"You heard what?'' he asked, begging off purient punishment.

"We heard y'all fuckin', Mose replied, in a breathy undercurrent voice, "she wouldn't gimme none o' that pussy 'til after she had her first baby.''

He walked for miles, feeling depressed. If I stay here, I'll be participating in this shit. "Shit! I'm already participating.'' He wound up on Peach Tree Street, strollilng up one side of the street and down the other, looking at the computer world. Somehow it seemed totally crazy that he would be living in the middle of a jungle and could walk a few blocks away from it. What the hell as I going through? This is the way things are. I can leave a place where people have decided not to have a Masters of Ceremony, not to superimpose any bullshit between themselves and the bullshit.

He ate a good Southern supper and strolled back to his "Jungle," feeling one-hundred percent more capable of dealing with his feelings about the scene. He measured/analyzed the laser beam looks as he slowly strolled up to the veranda. There was a section of hostile eyes (Coffee, Thimble, a face) who didn't like him because he had gotten something that they wanted. Or something that they had once had and wanted more of. Or simply those who resented him because he was doing something they couldn't do. Or hadn't done.

May Lou stood up from her position between Coffee and Thimble as he mounted the stairs past Mose. "Evenin', Chester."

He felt tempted to simply nod to her greeting but he knew it wouldn't be appropriate. When a Black woman in the South gave you some pussy, and she wasn't a 'hoe, you had to acknowledge her. "Evenin', May Lou."

He was already packed when he heard the tapping on his door. She was an hour late, it was four a.m. Beautiful woman, a creature of costumes, she was wearing a black raincoat over nothing.

"May Lou."

"Looks like you goin' somewhere, Chester."

He sat in the dilapidated chair, watching her take half steps around his room. She knew he was leaving her intrinsically good pussy, three men had already done it, including her natural father.

"Chester, you get high?"

"I got a pint of Beefeater gin on the dresser over there."

"Nawww, I ain't talking 'bout gin, gettin' drunk. I'm talkin' bout gittin' high."

A half hour later, under the influence of some 'erb that had been grown in the rich-red clay earth of Georgia, he poured himself a thimble full of Beefeater in a coffee cup and watched May Lou's gesture-dance-speech about what she took to be the inevitable result of her love life.

"You know, I sometime be thinkin'...somethin' got to be wrong with you, May Lou, all these mens want some o' yo' pussy, but don't nobody wanna stay with you."

"May Lou..."

"I mean, it be a thing like, hey, what I'm 'sposed to be, free pussy or somethin', huh?"

"May Lou..."

"Don't git all twisted outta shape, I ain't talkin' about you, I'm talking 'bout the dudes who be comin' up on me, talkin' 'bout how fine they think I is 'n whatnot."

"May Lou..."

"Like my first baby's father. I was almost a virgin when he got me pregnant. 'May Lou, I luv you.' That's what he said. Y'hear what I'm sayin'?" They passed the joint back and forth a couple times. "Yeahhh, I luved the little ol' poot butt. I knew he wadn't inta nothin', but I luved him y'hear what I'm sayin'?"

He had reacted the nodding stage, there was nothing to say.

"Now if you really wanna hear the Gospel truth, I wadn't even in luuv with my second baby's father. I was just sho' nuff in heat. My momma told me, 'May Lou, yo' nature just comin' down on you. You don't need no man, you need'ta git yo' ass outta heah 'n go to a school or find yourself a job.' But nawww, I was too knot-headed to listen t' Momma. I was twenty years old'n I knew everything." The eruption of a noise that sounded like grenades exploding caused her to pause for a moment. "Cherie's father really fooled me. He was one o' them Cre'alls from Naw 'Leans, a pretty man. He was the kind who thought women came just 'cause he'd stuck it up in there." She smiled at the puzzled look on Chester's face. "You know, a lotta pretty men be thinkin' that, just 'cause they put it in, you gotta be satisfied."

117

Chester, high on high-grade Georgia 'erb and the urge to get one last piece of this 'essentially good pussy', broke into the monologue.

"What satisfies you?"

"I don't really know. But I can tell you this, having a man drop a load off in me don't automatically gimme no pleasure. I started payin' 'ttention to things like that since my momma had me git my tubes tied."

Dawn, and the spring heat that was gradually broiling into early summer, found them coiled around each other like snakes.

"Chester, you know somethin'?"

"What, May Lou?"

"If you wasn't so old and you wasn't so weird 'n stuff, I'd be in luuve with you."

"And if you weren't so scarred by your life, I'd be in love with you."

He boarded the morning bus to Augusta, half high and drunk, feeling in hopeless love with a woman named May Lou, knowing that he need a smaller, more peaceful environment to do "Simone" in.

"Chester, you comin' back to see me?"

"May Lou, if I came back to see you, I'd have to stay with you."

The hurt look she stunned him with lasted until he reached the outskirts of Augusta, Georgia, The Garden City.

Chapter 16

Augusta is the second largest city in Georgia, after Atlanta, and half a dozen people had told him good things about it.

"Shit, I'd move back to 'Gusta in a minit if my job wasn't here."

"It's a pretty little town, green everywhere."

Fort Gordon was just up the road from the city, but there wasn't an overwhelming military presence hanging over the city. It was twelve o'clock, high noon, when he stepped from the coolness of the airconditioned bus into the steambath humidity of Augusta. He had been given enough info about the city, from Della Mae Jones herself, to be able to go places.

"Excuse me, could you tell me how to get to the Red Star Hotel?"

The middle-aged Black man wrestling the luggage from the bowels of the bus straightened up to point the way. "This here's Green Street here. Walk down that way fo' blocks, turn right on Vernon and keep walkin' 'til you come to the Red Star. You cain't miss it. Hits jest befo' you get to the railroad tracks.''

The perspiration ran down the creases in his back, formed half moon pockets under his arms, made his shorts wet and gummy. "Damn, it's hot . . ." Eight sweaty blocks after his right on Vernon, he staggered into the Red Star Hotel.

In comparison to Della Mae Jones' rooming house, the Red Star Hotel rated four stars. Or maybe ten. He paused inside the entrance. Thank God for airconditioning . . .

The interior was red carpeted, cool, the wood was polished. The windows were crystal clean, the atmosphere genteel.

"Can I help you, sir?"

The well modulated female voice came from behind a well-polished counter five yards to his right; he hasn't noticed it when he staggered in. He hefted his luggage over to the counter.

"I'd like a room"

The desk clerk, a small, tailored brown-skinned woman turned the registration book around for his signature. "Double or single?" she asked as he scribbled his name, trying not to let the moisture from his hand blot the page.

"Uhh, that'll be a single. It's awfully humid today, isn't it?"

She smiled up in his face, revealing dimples on each side of her mouth. "You should've been here last week. Are you planning to be with us awhile, uhh, Mr. Simmons?"

He glanced around the establishment. It was clean, cool and quiet, a good place to write. "At least a month anyway."

She made a note beside his name. "Good. We'll try to make your stay at the Red Star as comfortable as possible. Would you like a front or rear room?

An hour later, after a cold shower, he stood in front of

120

the window of his room, a gin and tonic in hand, his cotton robe on, looking down at the slow moving bunches of people. I'll have to get out there when the sun goes down, get an idea of what the deal is. It took him a half hour at nine p.m., strolling up and down Broad Street to come to the conclusion that there was not a lot happening out there. Families, Black and white, window shopped; paused for double dips of Rocky Road, enjoyed the coolness of the night air. The town was socially divided, as in most American cities, by the railroad tracks. The main stem in the white section was Broad Street, Gwinnett-Laney in the Black section of town.

Broad Street was where the shops were, the Power. Gwinnett Street was where the Black barber shop, the funeral home, the library and the liquor store was.

He slept the sleep of the innocent, lulled into dreams by the distant sound of a train whistle.

Augusta was an easy place to live in. There was a minimum of tension between the races; Mr. and Mrs. Robeson, the Red Star owners, explained: "We used to have lots of problems with these crackers, back in the bad ol' days, but some of 'em woke up 'n smelled the coffee. They were losin' too much money to continue to try to keep the Black folks down."

And a sense of tradition seemed to prevent wild and woolly things from taking hold. There seemed to be no roving herds of gangs, like Chicago, Los Angeles or Atlanta. And people seemed to genuinely care about each other. Chester was practically taken by the hand, on more than one occasion, after he had wandered too far afield, and placed gently back onto the track. "Now stay right on this street 'til you come to Maybelle's Restaurant, turned left at that corner and then keep on 'til you come to a sign that say...awww, tell ya what, I ain't got nothin' better to do. I'll show you. You say you from El-A, huh? I had a cousin move out there duin' the wah. Helluva place, that's what he told me, helluva place..."

The Red Star Hotel was his base of operations and Augusta became his southern version of Alicante. The Robesons became his friends after his second month of residency. "So, you're a writer. That's good. Our race needs writers, people who have enough vision and intelligence to be able to explain the meaning of this life to us."

The Red Star Hotel dining room, famous for its Friday fish dinners, is where he saw her first. He had been having an unusually difficult time, struggling with "Simone's" reasons for not becoming a 'modern woman.' *I don't see the purpose in being a so-called modern woman, if what I read in the magazines and what I see on the streets is any indication of what a modern woman is supposed to be.*

It wasn't exactly writer's block. This struggle that he was making to have a fictional character (who represented reality) define her role in life, but it bordered on a block. He had re-written five pages three times when he decided to put it on hold. *Maybe one of these Red Star fish dinners will show me the way.*

"Evenin', Mr. Simmons. Glad you decided to come down for dinner. Gloria is fryin' catfish tonight."

He had his own table near the rear, that allowed him to eat and observe. He had become one of the regulars, which meant he would strike up a conversation with the people near him, or eat and quietly sip a beer and not be bothered. The quiet, efficient bustle that seemed to characterize the Robeson operation on every level, was in effect. The dining room, almost a complete throwback to the days when people surrounded themselves with fine woods, lace curtains and snow white table cloths, was full. He nodded to familiar faces and took his seat. Stella Robinson, the fifteen year old, materialized with a frosted glass and a bottle of Heineken dark. They knew his tastes. "Evenin', Mr. Simmons. Will you be havin' the catfish dinner?"

"Sho' will, Stella. And peach cobbler for dessert." Chester smiled to himself in the beautifully lit room. Damn, I'm beginning to sound like I was born here. He gazed around the room, his mind on "Simone," admiring the subdued lighting. Mrs. Robeson was responsible for that. "I hate to go into restaurants with all that harsh lighting, it makes the food look ugly."

She entered the dining room like a fawn, stepping surely but carefully. The undercurrent hum of the dining room conversations seemed to fade away as she stopped and looked around. Mrs. Nadine Robeson was at her side immediately, they were obviously friends.

He stared across the room at her, taking in the slow gestures, the way her mouth moved as she talked. God, what a beautiful woman.

His writer's eye for details made an effort to single out some specific feature, to focus on. A part of her that singularly defined her beauty.

"God, what a beautiful woman."

She was being led to his table by Mrs. Robeson. "Uhhh, Mr. Simmons, we seem to have a rare problem, here . . ." He stood and concentrated on making the most suave speech he could make, without trying to sound flirty.

"Mrs. Robeson, it would be my pleasure to share this table with this beautiful lady."

"That's very gracious of you," she said in a clear low tone.

"Mr. Chester Simmons, Miss Valaida Hurston." They shook hands and she sat down opposite him. "Mizz Hurston is in charge of our library," Mrs. Robeson spoke over her shoulder as she moved away to serve a customer. The low-beamed chandelier behind her framed her head in a halo.

"So, you're a librarian?"

"Yes, I am." Her smile was fleeting, but honest.

She must be about forty, very intelligent, beautiful sense of humor. Close up, studying the laugh lines at the corners of her eyes, he could better understand why he couldn't pull out a single element and focus on that. Physically, she was beautiful, shapely, but that seemed to be almost a nonessential element of her beauty. She would probably be a beautiful woman with crooked teeth and a bump on her nose. There was a sense of beauty about her that made her beautiful. He felt oddly at ease with her, not compelled to fill the space with chit-chat. She nodded to a couple across the room, sprinkling her fingers in the air the way that well bred southern Black women did, whenever they greeted friends at a distance.

Stella Robeson glided over with a glass of water. "Hi, Miss Hurston, you're havin' the catfish?"

"I certainly am. I've been lookin' forward to it all week. How's that reading list going?"

"Pretty well. I'm about two books ahead of schedule now."

"That's good, Stella, really good."

"Yes, m'am."

He was intrigued by her voice, the sultry quality of it. She gave the Southern accent a distinct flavor. "I wish my neighborhood librarian had been as interested in my reading when I was growing up."

Once again, she cast a fleeting smile in his direction. He wasn't certain but he had the feeling that she didn't want to become involved in a conversation, just for the sake of filling in space. He sipped his beer.

The catfish dinners were placed in front of them. Mr. Daniel Robeson made a circuit of the room, pausing here and there to exchange words with the regulars. He leaned

124

over their table, more a gracious host welcoming guests, than a hotel-restaurant owner. "And how're you folks this evenin'?" They mumbled satisfied sounds in his direction as he smiled at them. "Good, I'm glad. Nadine was tellin' me what happened. Looks like this is one of those Friday nights when everybody wanted some catfish. She had me laughin', talkin' 'bout what a coincidence it was that she would wind up seatin' the librarian with the writer. Well, enjoy your dinner now." Mr. Robeson moved on to the next table, "And how're you folks doin' this evenin'?"

"What do you write about, Mr. Simmons?"

He felt slightly uneasy for the first time since she'd been seated across from him. It was always difficult because he had gotten into it so late in life. But aside from that, he felt self-conscious and that it was a little pretentious. He decided to be as brief and direct as possible. "I'm making an effort to write about life as I see it, hopefully from a perspective that will offer my readers a deep understanding of themselves."

The fleeting smile lingered a bit and she looked into his eyes for a long moment. "That sounds like a mighty ambitious undertakin'."

It was his turn to smile. "It certainly is, believe me."

She accepted his suggestion that she have peach cobbler for dessert. "I don't need much promptin' when it comes to eating Gloria Robeson's cooking." She obviously enjoyed good food, obviously wasn't concerned about gaining weight. He guessed her to be about a hundred-and-twenty-five, well-organized pounds, and knew how to preserve her sense of privacy. One of the things he had noticed about the Augustans was their sharply defined sense of propriety. No one in the Red Star Hotel had questioned him about where he came from, what he was doing in Augusta, or where he was going after he left. He was the one who had revealed that he was a writer, that he had recently returned from Europe and that he was currently writing a book.

She was placing her napkin beside her plate and pushing her chair back to stand up before he fully realized she was leaving.

"Thank you for sharing your table with me, Mr. Simmons, and I wish you all the best with your work."

He stood and shook her hand. What else was there to do? He held onto her hand for a beat or two too long. "It was my pleasure, Miss Hurston."

There were five important questions on the back of his tongue that he couldn't ask. When will I see you again? Would you give me your phone number, I'd like to call you? Are you married? No, you couldn't be, married women didn't have dinner alone, in the Red Star Hotel dining room. Where do you live? Who are you, really?

He made an effort to cast his eyes down demurely as she moved away from the table. It would never do for people to see him staring lasciviously at this beautiful woman's gorgeous hips like a common man of the streets.

He returned to his room, showered and sprawled across the bed, "Simone" eclipsed by Valaida Hurston. He laced his hands behind his head and stared up at the flickering lights on the ceiling. The always distant hooting of trains and the throb of the Georgia summer lulled him into a light sleep.

She turned to him and smiled her quick smile. He wrapped her in his arms and hugged her naked body to him. They were in a sun-drenched forest of ferns, flowers of all kinds waving at them, luscious scents. She spoke, her voice sliding up and down the tonal scale, musically, "Chester Simmons, how can you say you love me and mean it. You only just met me yesterday?"

"I can say it, I am saying it and I do love you and it doesn't matter whether it was yesterday or in the Ice Age when we

126

met. Don't you understand that?''

He heard himself moan just before waking up. He looked down at his erect penis, held it in his fist for a minute. What's the deal? Do I simply want to fuck this outrageously fine sister, or is it something else? He sat up on the side of the bed, channeling his head back to the story of ''Simone.'' I'm definitely going to have to find out who this lady really is.

Chapter 17

Stella Robeson, "Mizz Hurston is the librarian. She's nice, too, she'll help you find anything you need."

Mrs. Nadine Robeson, "Valaida Hurston and I went to school together. She's really a lovely person, isn't she?"

Mr. Daniel Robeson, "Hah, hah, hah . . . well, what can I say to you, Chester? Valaida Hurston is almost as big a mystery to us homefolks as she is to you. She's not one to spell her lifestory out for the public to read."

Chester, "Is she married?"

Mr. Daniel Robeson, "Now that I do know. Nope, she ain't married. Husband got killed in a car accident 'bout three years ago. Kinda like that firewater a lil' bit too much, if you know what I mean."

He assembled bit and pieces, in search of the whole thing and wound up with larger bits and pieces. In the middle of the afternoon, three days later, taking a nap after a sunrise struggle to make chapter eight believable, he popped up.

The library! She's in the library!

He showered and shaved hurriedly, as though he were keeping an appointment. She's in the library . . .

He grabbed a notebook and a couple ballpoints on the way out, something to make his visit look legitimate. "Uhh, ahhem, 'scuse me, Mrs. Robeson, could you direct me to the library?"

She peeked over the top edge of her glasses, reminding him of Ife Ebuni for a moment. "Well, we have two within walkin' distance. There's the main library and there's the branch library, the one we call 'our library'. The slightest hint of a smile played into the corners of her mouth. "Which one do you want to go to?"

He recognized the game she was playing with his head, but he didn't have any idea what the boundries were. "Uhhh, I kinda think that what I want is in 'our library'."

The hint of a smile broadened. "Walk over to Gwinnett Street and turn right. You can't miss it."

He rushed out into the humid streets, walking fast enough to be identified as a tourist. The natives knew better than to move quickly when the temperature was in the nineties and the humidity was almost as high. His short-sleeved shirt was stuck to his back by the time he pulled the doors of the branch library open and perspiration ran down both sides of his face. He paused inside the entrance, wiping perspiration from his brow and offering thanks to the great lord technology for airconditioning. He stopped a young man with black horn rims. "'Scuse me, young blood, can you direct me to the men's room?"

The owlish looking young man, obviously a habitual visitor to the library, "It's around the corner, to your left."

Chester wanted to splash a little cold water on his face, comb his hair, brace himself up a bit before coming face to face with Valaida Hurston again.

He bumped into her turning the corner.

"Oh, Miss Hurston, sorry!"

She acknowledged his apology with a curt nod and glided past him. He stood in place for a moment, sweaty, puzzled. "Damn, she acted like she didn't even know me." He splashed cold water on his face in the toilet and stared at himself in the mirror. She certainly knows how to punch a guy in the ego, that's for sure. He wandered around the small library, going in and out of the stacks until he came up on her in one of the aisles replacing books. "Ah hah, Miss Hurston, we meet again." He felt certain for a moment, that she wasn't going to acknowledge him.

"Oh, Mr. Simmons, I thought that was you that I almost ran over a few minutes ago but I wasn't sure. I'm almost as blind as a bat without my glasses. What brings you to our library?"

He felt like screaming, "You brought me to your library, Valaida Hurston! You brought me here!"

"Oh, just doin' a little research. The book I'm working on now . . ."

"Well, if you need any assistance, just let me know." She moved down the aisle with her cart full of books. She was obviously not given to long social conversations. He stood there, dry and cool now, his notebook clutched uselessly in his hand, feeling frustrated. He felt almost as frustrated with himself as he felt with her. He sat at one of the tables, thumbed through a *National Geographic,* tried to objectively analyze his feelings. Okay now, Chester Simmons, let's be for real here. You dig the lady, right? Yes, I do dig her. But how do you dig her, is it simply a physical turn on, a tits 'n ass sensation? Someone you want to work on jones with? What? He closed the magazine and stared out of the picture window at Black, slow moving, energy saving Augusta. I want to get to know this woman, have a

130

relationship with her, of some kind. Who knows? We could wind up being simply friends. No, scratch that. I don't see a platonic thing happened. We'd have to become lovers. I'm positive of that. But how is any of this going to happen, under the circumstances.

He knew he was up against a host of odds. The Red Star Hotel was his 'home' and the Robesons were like family but so far as they were concerned and the other regulars he'd met he was still a foreigner, a friendly foreigner, but a foreigner nevertheless. He realized, for the first time since his arrival, that the friendliness, the warmth was sincere, but measured. They gave off good vibes, but only up to a certain point. He had to design an outline that would take it past smiles and "Hi-you-this-moanin's" level.

"Well, I suppose the writer has to do a heap of thinkin' before he begins to put pen to paper, doesn't he?"

"Oh?"

"Sorry, didn't mean to startle you."

"Oh, no, no, you didn't. I was just thinking. Yes, you're right, a lot of thought does go into it."

She sprinkled a graceful wave at him and danced away to handle a book checkout. The woman seemed to be in motion even when she's sitting in one place. He had replayed their dinner through his head a dozen times, and each time, he recalled, when he had reached the point of saying something personal to her, she had fled. It was purely an illusion, he knew that, but the effect of the illusion was real. He stood up to leave, a decision made to return to his room and put a plan, an outline together.

Her parting remark to him as he passed the checkout desk sounded like a challenge. "Evenin' Mr. Simmons, hope you found what you wanted?"

"I do, too," he answered and waved goodbye.

131

Chapter 18

"Simone" is kickin' my ass. He rifled through the pages he had written and then flipped through the pages he wanted to write. The future is definitely ahead of the past. Maybe I'm drinking too much. He took a long pull on his third gin 'n tonic. Gin seemed to be exactly the right liquid for the heat, for his frustration. It was clear, it had a sharp taste and when he had enough of them, he could go to sleep without replaying his anxiety type.

"Simone" is really kicking my ass...

He was beginning to have doubts about his reasons for writing about a woman. What the hell do I know about being a woman? He reread his first 110 pages and came to the conclusion that he knew quite a lot about women, but there was something missing, an element that he couldn't put his finger on. Why didn't I sell Franklin House the idea of something else? Why would I stick my neck into this kind of noose? O well...

It was Friday again, the dinner hour was an hour away. He had done his homework. She's off at five p.m. and she's here to have one of Gloria's catfish dinners by five-forty-five p.m. He showered and dressed casually, but carefully; a cocoa tie-dyed sports shirt and white linen pants. He swallowed a double shot of Beefeaters, neat and took one last look at himself in the mirror. Are y'all ready for Chester L. Simmons, also known as the great lawd Buddha?

The dining room was three-fourths full when he arrived. "Mrs. Robeson, will you be kind enough to escort Mizz Hurston to my table when she arrives?" Mrs. Robeson, the most discreet of discreet hotel owners, didn't blink.

"I sho' will, Mr. Simmons."

He strutted to his table, nodding and smiling to the regulars, feeling a little high and cocky. Damn, I've been tip-toeing around here like I was some sort of funky chump. "Fuck that, I'm Chester Louis Simmons, sheeeit."

He was beginning to understand the Friday night tradition between Friday nights. He glanced around at the man who was with a different woman than he was with the first time he saw him. And at his female counterpart.

The dining room was a short story writer's heaven; the definitely older man with the barely legal age females, both of them drunk on the thought of the after dinner feast. The older woman with her slightly younger girlfriend, catfish dinners for two years now. The lovely, loving family, all of them enjoying everything. No wonder they don't want to show the real Black family on television. It wasn't the cute little kid (per TV) cracking the family up. It was the great-greatgrandfather, ninety years old, slipping hip quips in between bits, "This catfish is screamin', y'all heah me, hits screamin'! Uhh huh."

Stella Robeson placed his frosted Heineken and glass in front of him and glided off to other duties. He sipped his beer, distracted by his thoughts, attracted to what he was seeing. So much love, so much love, people huggin' 'n kissin' on each other, puttin' food into each others mouths, enjoying each others company.

"You left directions that I should be escorted to your table, Mr. Simmons?"

He did a perfect double take and felt slightly embarrassed at being caught gathering moss. "Yes, please, sit down."

Smart blue suit, no nonsense purse, ruffled white shirt front, a business person. She sat as requested and leaned back in the chair like a queen. The look challenged him. It said, "Awright, you've invited me to your table, I'm here, now what?" The room suddenly became smaller and there was only the two of them. He sipped his beer and studied her.

Aristocratic, that was the other word that described her. Beautiful aristocrat. A natural queen that no one had crowned. He was beginning to understand the emotional make up of many Black women. God, if they hadn't reminded themselves that they were queens, I wonder what would've happened?

Stella, the waitress, interrupted their silent exchange by taking their orders. "The catfish dinner, like everybody else?" They turned to nod in unison. And then slowly turned back to stare in each others eyes.

"You don't talk a lot, do you?"

"No, I don't. Do you?" She had a classy way of turning him around on himself.

"Only when I have something to say."

"Well, what do you have to say?"

They leaned their elbows on the table and looked closely into each others eyes. He saw shiny spots in her eyes, a rational gleam. How can I make it sound like the truth? Don't even try, just let it out.

"I'm interested in you. I've only seen you two times

134

before, three with this meeting, this dinner and I'm simply attracted to you. I don't know if you're married, or have a lover or what. But I do know that I'd be misrepresenting myself if I told you that I wasn't interested in you.''

She turned away to stare at a distant point. He felt panicked for a moment. *Did I go too far too soon?*

''You know, it's strange how things can be,'' she spoke, still eyeing the distant point. ''The last time I sat at this table with an old family friend, friend to me 'n my husband before his accident, he said to me, I never will forget it, 'Valaida, I dreamed that my dick was in your pussy last night.'''

He recoiled involuntarily. This statement was so gross that it didn't even seem as though it came from her mouth. She smiled at his reaction, a broad, lingering smile. ''Oh please, Mr. Simmons, don't pretend to be shocked. You're a man of the world, you know how men are . . .''

They had their catfish. She refused a beer and ordered tea. They began to tease each other. ''You know, where I come from, only bar girls order tea.''

''Well, that spares them the burden of alcoholic addiction, doesn't it''

''That's not the worst vice in the world.''

''What is?''

''Being addicted to hate, and not love.''

She liked the slash and jab of rapier conversation, being ahead of where he was going and waiting there to ambush him. ''But don't you see, Mr. Simmons?''

''The name is Chester, please.''

''All right. What I'm saying is simple. Things are not what they seem to be.''

''Ain't that the truth.'' She laughed from the gut. The aristocrat was down to earth, a long way from being the person that her image conveyed. There were six people, besides themselves, dawdling over coffee and a last spoon of rice pudding, before he noticed.

"Looks like we're the last ones in the house."

She slouched back in her seat. "I've really enjoyed talkin' with you, Mr. Simmons."

"Is it over?" He loved the look, it was always a question and a challenge. She pushed her chair back and stood up. A beige colored woman. He had been trying to find the color label for her, not to define her, but to know the shade of woman he was so intrigued by.

"It's over in the Red Star Hotel dining room," she pointed her chin at young Stella Robeson, half asleep behind the cash register, "Native Son" open in front of her.

He insisted that he pay for their dinners. She protested.

"Mr. Simmons!"

"Chester!"

"Chester, you're under no obligation to pay for my dinner."

"I know," he told her, and paid. They strolled out into the Friday night street. They stood in front of the hotel for a minute, trying to decide what to do. "I'd like to drive you home, but I don't have a car."

The fleeting smile swept across his eyes. "I don't live far from here. I usually walk home." They strolled across the tracks, walled in by darkness and a million insect sounds, the South.

"You know something, Valaida?"

"What?"

"I feel closer to my feelings down here, in the South."

"Many of us do, Chester, I think it has something to do with the West African climate."

He wanted to put his arm ever so gently around her waist and squeeze her to him, but he controlled himself. What if she only thinks I'm only tryin' to cop a piece of stray trim? But what are you after? he asked himself. Not pussy, God no, not from her. I'd have to want everything she is. His nose was open and he knew it.

"We're here. I can invite you in for a cup of tea or coffee, but you'll have to leave in a few minutes because I don't want to set a bad example for the young women in the neighborhood. After all, remember, this is a small community and people do talk, you know how it is?"

He decided to skip the amenities and kissed her on her front doorstep, amidst the magnolia bushes.

"Why, Mr. Simmons!"

He felt like he was in an English drawing room comedy. Was she going to slap his face? "Should I apologize for wanting to kiss you?"

"No, but what's going to happen afterwards?" She was talking about commitment. His hands began to sweat.

"Afterwards"

"After my neighbors have seen me necking on my doorstep with a strange man." He couldn't tell if she were joking or not, for a beat. She was joking.

"You're not concerned about your neighbors, are you?"

"No," she said, "I'm not really concerned about them. I'm concerned about me, about my feelings." She fell up against him with such force that he almost tumbled over. This woman was filled with surprising stuff. She pressed her body against him and placed her lips on his. She wasn't a good kisser. But she was into the feeling. He could tell that. They stood there, pressed together for ten minutes and then she pulled away from him, stuck her key in the door, raced inside, "Good night, Chester Simmons."

He walked away from her front door, feeling excited, mystified, happy. "Chester, you foxy ol' motherfucker you, you're in love with this incredible creature. Yes, Lawd, I am in love."

His days changed, his life was transformed. "Simone"

began to have a shape. "Simone" was Valaida Hurston.

Valaida Hurston had been married to a man who didn't know how to love and had stuck in there like a well-trained bullpit terrier. She believed in 'till death do us part.' And her husband's death had pulled them apart, given her a release. She had been celibate for three years and would've been content to remain that way if Chester hadn't put in an appearance. They became a Black community item: "Noted author, Chester Simmons, and Ms. Valaida Hurston were in attendance at the opening of the African-American Center for Culture and Prosperity." Chester was amazed at the phenomenon of family around him suddenly. Ms. Valaida Hurston was connected to the town, the town to her. Chester suddenly discovered that he was on display. People were paying attention to him. How many writers did they have in town who had been published? He couldn't hang out in the low places he'd found out about in Augusta because it would've reflected badly on the librarian.

He loved the adulation, but it didn't produce any orgasms.

"Valaida, look, we're adults, who would care if we made love?"

"We would care, Chester, and that's the point. I'm not one of your modern women, who jump in and out of bed with every man who's attracted to me."

He wandered home from her place, night after night, past couples glued to each other in the shadows of porches and front yard trellises, feeling more and more sex starved. Shy Gloria Robeson, who cooked the wonderful catfish dinners that pulled everybody into the Red Star dining room was almost a beneficiary of his frustration. Gloria the cook, everybody called her, was the oldest of the two Robeson daughters (twenty-six years old). Chester first noticed her eyes through the slit that the plates of food were passed through. He painted mental pictures of the body underneath these large, lustrous black eyes, framed in dark shadows and sweat. He was loyal to Valaida, but Gloria's eyes disturbed him. He had to be extremely careful. Single men of a certain age (his age), were thought to be lower than dogs if they ran from woman to woman. And it was a known fact that Chester was Valaida's man.

"Do I really want to get married and settle down here?"

Gloria, dark eyes in the kitchen slit, was plump and earthy and horny. Chester discovered her urge walking up the back stairs one afternoon. He had been jogging in a nearby park, that was more like a swamp than a park. He was sweaty, funky and feeling loose. She was standing on the back porch, leaning on the railing, killing time.

"I saw you over there on the track. How many laps do you do?"

"About ten. You're Gloria, aren't you? I recognize your eyes."

"My eyes?"

"Yeahhh, you know, that's all we can see when you're in the kitchen."

"I be seein' you too, in the dinin' room," she spoke as though she had been paying as much attention to him as he had been paying to her eyes. An awkward moment struggled by. The girl was built, no doubt about that. I'd be blind not to notice that. She was just at the perfect point of plumpness. In six months, he estimated, she'd burst open like a grape and balloon to some unknown shape. She straightened up and flexed her left leg in his direction.

"Uhhh, you really fry a helluva catfish, you know that?"

She looked disappointed and leaned back over the railing. She sounded almost bitter as she spoke. "That's all people ever talk to me about is cookin'." He felt like folding her into his arms and whispering, "I didn't mean to ignore your feelings. I know what it's like to be alone. Doin' what you love to do, but still alone."

"Look, Gloria, I'm all sweaty. I gotta take a shower."

"Go'head, I'm not stoppin' you, am I?" She looked so pretty, with her bottom lip stuck out.

Valaida had practically eliminated the idea of other women in his life. Her impact was that strong. He glanced quickly at Gloria's buttocks on the way past.

"This sister has got a nice set of buns on her."

Chapter 19

He was coming to the end of "Simone" and "Simone" had become Valaida Hurston. He had to re-write large sections of the piece after opening himself to the revelations that Valaida laid on him.

"Chester, don't you understand? Women are more romantic than men. Men are almost exactly like bulls, or male gorillas, or what have you. I'm not saying that to cast aspersions on the bulls or the gorillas..."

"You've made your point perfectly clear. You want to make love to me but you're afraid that it might spoil something, right?"

"No, I'm afraid that I might just simply wind up being another one of your conquests."

"Valaida, haven't I told you that I love you?"

"Chester, you are going to try to convince me that you've never told a woman that you love her?" She stumped his efforts to be glib, to make it too simple.

141

"Valaida, do you know that I think of you all the time?"

"And I think of you all the time, too but that is not going to create a successful, intimate relationship between us." She was a librarian and he sometimes felt that she had read too many novels from the Victorian era. She was sexy, but didn't realize it, he discovered.

"Valaida, how do you feel when you go places and people stare at you?"

"People staring at me, when?"

Her life had been governed by order, dignity, her relationship to her husband, it seemed. "Tom was an old-fashioned man. He didn't believe in showing too much emotion. I'm sure he loved me, but he never told me that, outright." He felt that she had missed too much and wanted to help her make up for lost time. They argued about it.

"Chester, what are you doin', tryin' to make me feel guilty for having slept with only one man in my life?" She had grown children who were invited home to inspect him (he felt) and they shared her sense of humor. Norene, the twenty-two year old computer whiz, quizzed him about his intentions. "What's the deal with you, Mr. Simmons. Are you plannin' to elope with my mother, or what?"

The two boys were equally straight forward. "Be careful how you handle this lady, sir. She is the only momma we've ever had."

He compulsively surrendered to his own secret urges and public opinion. "Valaida, I want to share my life with you. I want you to be my wife."

"O, my Gawd, Chester! Behave yourself. You don't want to be stuck down here with a straight-laced, inexperienced, middle-aged woman who has not seen anything, done anything or been anywhere."

"I think those are some of the reasons I love you and I want to marry you."

"Let me think about it for a couple weeks. Why don't we both think about it?" She shushed his romantic protests and, as usual, escorted him to the door at eleven p.m. "Be careful, Chester. There was a rumor about a lady gettin' her purse snatched the other night."

During the course of the two week 'cool off' period, he explored every negative aspect of his proposal. I'm too old and set in my ways to have a marriage with anyone. Ol' Patcheye used to say, remember, Chester, there's a lawnmower attached to marriage. She's too old and set in her ways to have a marriage with anyone. I hate the idea of settling down, or living in one place for the rest of my life. This means the end of my acknowledged pursuit of other women. What can I do with her that I couldn't do by myself? What if she isn't what she really seems to be? What effect will she have on my work?

He re-wrote the ending for "Simone" three times, trying to see all of the possibilities that might occur in the life of a woman he had modeled after a real person.

"Yes, Chester, I would like to be your wife, but, to be perfectly honest with you, I think you love me more than I love you." He did a double-take and decided to go with the flow.

Their wedding was the "in" event of the winter season.

"That's just like Valaida, ain't it? To get married in the coldest month of the year."

"Anybody know anything about Mr. Simmons?"

"He's supposed to be a world famous writer."

"I never heard of him."

"Me neither."

They moved into Valaida's home in the African-American section of town. Valaida didn't take any time off from work but they made love at least once a day for the first thirty-one days of their marriage.

"Chester, 'member you almost laughed in my face when I told you I was saving it for my next husband?"

"I'll never forget it, and you won't let me forget it, will you?"

"Was I worth waitin' for?" Chester's answer to her question often took them on marathon lovefests that started in the breakfast nook and ended in the bathtub. Or upstairs in the attic.

The Aristocratic Sister Hurston was the exact opposite of her image in private life, in her intimate life. "What two people do in their bedroom should be private and different, don't you agree?" She did lascivious hoochie koochie dances in the blue bulbed bedroom, wearing a blouse and bra. Or nothing. She teased him with the sight of her exposed breasts, sitting at the Sunday morning breakfast table.

"If men can walk around without shaving, women oughta be able to go without tops."

"What's the logic behind this? I don't see it."

They were sometimes silly with each other, mocking all of the stupidity that surrounded them.

"My goodness, Chester, look at that. You'd think the poor woman would've had enough sense not to be homeless in this neighborhood."

On the thirty-first day of their lovefest, the sprawled around in bed all day, reciting Kahlil Gibran and Langston Hughes, eating shrimp salad and drinking bottled water. The woman who had always held her head down when she met strangers, slowly revealed her poetic gifts.

"Chester, I don't really know what to think of this. Give me your opinion?"

He felt it was time to do the third draft, the final one, he promised himself. Franklin House committed themselves to a lucrative five book deal. Chester and Valaida had a flourishing lifestyle. It was 1990, it was the South, but it wasn't the ol' South. Or the Ol' North, for that matter. They were pleased that they had discovered each other.

"Chester, what is 'Simone' about?" He dodged her question for several days, raking the yard, painting a section of the backyard fence, being inconspicuous or unavailable. Finally, it wasn't possible for him to avoid her.

"Awww baby, 'Simone' is about a woman who wasn't the best-loved woman in the world, if you know what I mean."

"I have some notion of what that condition is like. What else do I have in common with this fictional character?"

"Not a lot. Remember, her name is Simone and yours is Valaida."

"Stop trying to be cute with me, Chester, I'm the well-read librarian, remember? Have you used me as the model for this piece?" He hugged her, he kissed her on both cheeks, did a boyish little shuffle, tried to evade answering the question. "Now, baby. What kind of question is that? Everybody can see themselves in what I write if that's who they're lookin' for. Sure, you might see resemblances here 'n there."

She wrestled with him on their bedroom floor, playfully, but serious. "Chester, this book better not be about me, you hear?"

During the course of their play periods, he found out some things that stunned him. He tiptoed up behind her in the kitchen, circling her waist from behind, nibbling on her ear. "You know, I'm glad I asked Mrs. Robeson to seat you at my table."

"I beat you to it."

"How's that?"

"I asked her to seat me at your table, the first time I saw you in the dining room."

"You did?"

"Yes, I sho' did. I spotted you when I first walked into the dining room, which is unusual for me because, as you know, I'm virtually sightless without my glasses. There was just something about you, a special kind of glow."

"Well, you know I was drinking a little gin at that point in time."

"Ohhh, I could tell you were a drinker and a carouser. I could definitely see that."

They tossed the issue of whether or not he was going to allow her to read the complete work back and forth a few times. They compromised.

"I can't let you read the whole thing, Valaida, it would spoil the published work for you."

"And just what makes you think that, Mr. Simmons?"

He became Mr. Simmons whenever she was not in total agreement with his attitudes. They re-compromised.

"Okay, tell you what. I'll give you the ending but you have to guess what the beginning is, okay?"

"Awww c'mon now, Chester Simmons, what kind of a deal is that?"

He folded his arms across his chest and put his stone face on. Matters were non-negotiable from this point.

"Alright, dahlin', have it your way."

They put a weekend aside for the reading of that last fifty pages, stocking up on pumpkin seeds and raisins.

"I know you think this is about you. I know you do."

"I'll soon find out, won't I?"

146

Chapter 20

He read slowly and feelingly. He had decided to do "Simone" as freely as he felt about her; stream-of-consciousness-non-punctuational-fuck-everything-style.

"'It always seemed to be autumn whenever anything happened to me. No matter what it was, if it had any impact at all it was something that happened in the fall of the year.

"'I was sold into marriage one fall evening. Sixteen and I was a virgin, a highly desirable item in those days. My husband was about fifteen years older than I was and had been married before.

"'I didn't love him (I hardly knew the man!) but my parents were pleased with him. I think I can understand why, now. I was sixteen, I was thought to be pretty and the young dogs, as we say down here, were beginning to sniff around my skirts. My parents had already been disgraced by my older sister, Katharine, who had had a baby out of wedlock.

"'You really have to understand what that was like back

then, 'specially for people of our class. We weren't rich, or even well-to-do. I think the best description would be classy lower middle class. But the economic designation didn't matter so much as our position in Augusta's Black society.

"'Father was a post office clerk, one of the first at that time and mother was a seamstress. He was a government employee, which meant that he didn't have to be concerned about whether his credit was going to be cut off at the company store. Or whether the boss might take a sudden dislike to him and fire him. He wasn't making boatloads of money but his job gave his family more security than most.

"'The upper crust white folks came to Mother with their gowns and they came respectfully because she was known to have a bad temper and wouldn't put up with any racial nonsense.

"'I can distinctly recall her dismissing at least three white women from the premises. One of them was the mayor's niece. The woman had said something about 'darkies' and Mother made her to understand that that kind of language was not tolerated in our home. That was the kind of respect they demanded from white folks, even back then, and they were granted that respect.

"'Sometimes, when I look back at those times, I have the feeling that I'm looking at ancient history. Can you imagine a Black family demanding and receiving respect from all sides? Nowadays, nobody respects anybody. Animals in the jungle show more respect for each other than we do.

"'Thomas Morton owned a funeral home and had a few acres of land that he leased. I guess you'd say he was wealthy. He used to make jokes about making his money off of the one thing white folks didn't want to touch, "I'm gon' always have me some money, 'long as Black folks die, 'cause white folks don't wanna have nothin' to do with us, 'specially when we dead and can't work for 'em no mo'."

"'Tom wasn't smart, bookwise, but he was shrewd and knew a lot about people. He had so much dirt on so many people that they were afraid to fool with him. He used to tell me stories (which I shall not repeat) about what Mr. So and So and Mizz So and So, and who had died in whose bed. Stuff like that.

"'Was I happy with him? I can't say that I was unhappy. He gave me everything I wanted and he wasn't a mean man. He liked to drink quite a lot, just like most of the men around here, but he never let that interfere with his work. I can remember him going to the funeral parlor to embalm somebody with his hands shaking from a hangover.

"'Yes, I did miss the romantic stuff, holding hands, whispering sweet nothin's into each others ears, little hugs and kisses, the flowers, movies. Frankly, Tom didn't understand that kind of behavior. He thought it was phoney. "That's movie star stuff. If a woman is well taken care of and her children provided for, that's what really matters. All the rest of that stuff is somethin' them people invented to try to keep people from feeling at ease with what they got."

"'I think that he was more 'real' to me than I was to him. I mean, he was down to earth, full of piss 'n vinegar and I was just sort of a frail little thing that he pounced on whenever the urge came over him. I hated our sex, our love life. I absolutely hated it. He would crawl in bed with me, that sour mash liquor on his breath, his hands still cold from cuttin' people open and sewin' 'em up. He would dig his big ol' rough fingers up in me a couple times and then he'd roll over on top of me.

"'I used to hint that he should go on a diet all the time, but he'd laugh in my face and eat a couple more pork chops. "Why the hell should I lose weight? There'd just be a little less of me to make money."

149

"'I had two children before I realized there was such a thing as an orgasm. And I wouldn't even have been aware of it, if it hadn't been for this perfectly outrageous nurse. Yes, of course, I had read of the female orgasm, but I hadn't had one. It was my second child, Clifford, and the nurse was bringing him to me for feeding.

"I bet you had a sweet nut for this one."

"Beg your pardon?"

"I just said, I bet you had a sweet nut for this one, y'know? 'Cause he's such a pretty baby." She sat by my bed, watching me nurse that gluttonous little demon. Clifford was always hungry. I was curious about her statement.

"What exactly is a sweet nut?" I think the woman must have stared at me for five minutes.

"Uhh, it'd be pretty hard to explain it to you, if you've never had one, honey."

"Go on, give it a try," I challenged her. And I'll never forget the moonbeam look that came into her eyes. She slumped back in this straight back chair beside my bed and closed her eyes for almost a minute.

"Well, first thing I have to say is that I've been told that this is different for different women."

"How was it, how was it for you?" I asked.

"Honey, when I cum sometimes it feels like a kind of hot wave sweeps over my whole body and the inside of my pussy is sweatin' some kind of delicious juice."

"'I'm not going to make any effort to explain to you how stunned I was when she started talking about her pussy sweatin' some kind of delicious juice. For all I was concerned, I could've been at a porno session or something, layin' there in bed, nursing my second born.

"I had one man," she told me, "who used to make me cum by suckin' my titties. I don't know what to say about him, I think he must've had special lips or something."

150

Sucking her titties! The closest Tom got to my breasts was to give them a kind of rough feel, from time to time.

"What else makes a woman, makes you cum?" I pressed her for as much information as I could get. I only had a few hours before my release.

"Well, I haven't heard tell of a woman who didn't respond positively to a good clit tonguin'."

"Clit tonguin'?" Once again, I swear to you, she actually sat there and stared at me.

"Honey, I'll be honest with you. I'm surprised that yo' pussy ain't been et completely out of socket."

"What makes you say that?"

"Are you serious? A beautiful sister like yourself?"

"But aside from all that, what's this clit tonguing?" I don't know, I'll never be able to say what was on her mind, whether she was a lesbian or whatever, but she must've taken pity on me to do what she did.

"Look, I'm gon' put my hands under the cover and place my fingertips on your clit, okay?" I must've nodded yes, with Clifford gurgling and slurping up all the milk he could get. I was almost paralyzed by an emotion I've never been able to explain, when I felt her fingers on my private area.

"This the first time I've ever done this," she explained to me, "and I don't really know what effect it'll have on you, what with you just having had a baby 'n all. And being shy." I felt almost like I was doing something dirty, you know what I mean? But not quite. After all, I was in a hospital bed, I'd just had a baby and the woman with her hand under the cover, fingering me, was a nurse in a white uniform. "You feel that?" I nodded, I was actually salivating from pleasure. I'll never forget it. "Now, that's your clit. It's like a miniature dick. How does that feel to you?"

"'She was giving me pure pleasure with her manipulations and I'm sure she knew it, but she didn't try to take advantage.

151

"Okay, now then, you know what your man be feelin' like when you do fellatio on him"

"When I do what?"

"You know, when you thrill his thriller." And she laughed aloud at the expression on my face. It was an instant trip from the Dark Ages to her Enlightened Era.

"When I thrill his thriller?"

"You mean you don't suck your ol' man's dick?"

"'Clifford gurgled off to sleep while I stared at her. "I've never seen my husband's penis."

"Well, honey, don't feel bad. Lots of women haven't. All I'm trying to say to you is this. You can feel just as much as he can feel, if you know how."

"You've lost me. How'm I gon' make myself feel like him? I may not know a bunch o' stuff, but I know that no woman is ever going to feel like a man, not when we come to lovemaking..."

"You're wrong, dead wrong. Women really have a greater capacity to enjoy it more because we have more stuff to work with. Can you feel this?" She was still fingering my clitoris and I was beginning to feel like I was going to float out of my skin.

"Uhh huh."

"Now then," she started off seductively, "can you imagine what you'd feel like if your husband, or boyfriend was playing around with your clitoris with his tongue?" I came. I would never be able to put my finger on what made it happen, but it did. No pun intended. I left the hospital after my second child feeling as though I had really discovered something. I immediately went to work, determined not to have another baby through the 'hole in the blanket,' as Nurse Shepherd put it. As soon as I was able I tried to introduce Tom to some of the things I'd been introduced to

"What're you doin'?"

"Just playin' with your thriller, baby."

"He recoiled from me with pleasure and fear. And it never really got any better than that. I had three children in three years, which shows how interested he was in me, but he never really made love to me and that was something I craved.

"I craved romantic life so desperately, I began to fantasize. I imagined myself being famous women in history, who had had fantastic love affairs. I reached the point of being able to fantasize so well that I could actually lose myself inside the covers of a book. I could become Cleopatra, Queen Nzingha, Catherine the Great, Mata Hari, the Queen of Sheba, Billie Holiday, Josephine Bonaparte, anyone I felt like, just by reading.

"I think it was about this time that I acquired the reputation for being cold and aloof. I didn't really matter all that much to me. As a matter of fact, it was better that way because it prevented people from prying into my private life. It's a cruel thing to realize, that you're not ever going to have the sweet, dreamy romantic life that girl's dream about. And I couldn't just go off and have an affair with some wild young stud. I was a nineteen year old married woman with three young children and that ruled out any kind of wild behavior on my part.

"I mean, what could I do, go down to the local bar and pick somebody up? Believe me when I say it, that was definitely not the thing to do at that time. So, I took refuge in the lives of the women that I read about in the history books. As Cleopatra, I could visualize myself floating down the Nile in a great barge, rowed by hundreds of slaves, bathing in camel's milk, my body being anointed with precious oils, cared for as though I were a unique creature on this planet.

"As Queen Nzingha, I could imagine myself as a warrior,

trying to defend her land against the foreign invaders.

"'I loved Catherine the Great because that gave me free play to be sexual, to allow myself to think the unthinkable. What would it be like to sleep with a regiment of men?

"'And so on. Sometimes, I spent weeks outside of myself, being someone else. I don't know how many people were directly affected by my behavior. I mean, to the extent that I was a disturbance to them. My children, bless their hearts, did a little fantasizing themselves, so I didn't think my behavior was a problem for them. They wanted a well-rounded Daddy as much as I wanted a well-rounded husband. Tom used to joke with his buddies about us. "My family is a bunch o' space cadets, y'know what I mean?" he was so, so, so dense! I tried to sit down and talk to him over the years, to explain that we needed more than a roof over our heads, clothes on our backs, money in the bank. "What more could you possibly need?" he'd ask me. And when I said, "Love," he'd stare at me like I had three heads. I could never get through to him Well, I should say I came close one time. It was in the autumn of 1985, never will forget it.

"'We were having one of those incredibly beautiful autumn days, the leaves were turning colors, the days were warm as your blood and sometimes night just seemed to fall on us like a blanket. You could tell that people were being affected by it from the way they were actin'. I caught Mr. and Mrs. Bradford, a couple who had been married since black pepper got its name, in the stacks down by the library, kissin' 'n feelin' on each other and everything.

"'Anyway, Tom came home from work early, the children were all off somewhere. "Baby," he says to me, "you know what? You sho' is a fine woman, you know that?" and then he kissed me, a long, tender kiss. Three days later, he was out driving, half drunk, and broadsided another car at the intersection of Bunker and Temple Street.

"'Suddenly, at thirty-seven years old, I was a widow with semi-grown up children and money in the bank. Yes, he had made provisions for us. I didn't know what to do with myself. I didn't belong to any organizations or anything because Tom had never approved of me going to meetings 'n stuff. And if the truth be told, I never had much patience for all that nonsense either. It all just seemed to be a waste of time, to have grown men and women sittin' around, runnin' their mouths and posturing.

"'I clearly recall what the 60s were like here in Augusta. It wasn't the speech makers and theorists who defeated segregation. It was the people who went out and did something about it. I didn't have any real close friends, if I discount the characters I used to fantasize about. Morene, my daughter, encouraged me to take a trip, "see the world." I thought about it for a bit before I vetoed the idea. I felt the money would be better spent on their college educations.

"'But Momma," they argued with me, "Daddy already set aside money for us to go to college."

"'After a year they finally persuaded me to take a two week trip to Chicago, to visit one of my female cousins. We're related to the writer Zora Neale Hurston, but I never like to broadcast that for fear that people will think you're trying to trade in on someone else's name.

"'My mother named me Valaida, after Valaida Snow, a famous Black lady trumpet player, singer and composer, who traveled all over the world and did fabulous things. I think that's why she gave me that name, as a kind of reminder that it was possible for a Black woman to do anything we had the nerve to do.

"'Anyway, I went off to Chicago, to Cousin Marva's. I'd never been North before and I didn't quite know what to expect. What can I say? I spent two weeks that were like a combination of everything you could imagine. Marva and I are about the same age but that's just about all we have in common. It started lookin' hairy from the minute she and her husband Robert picked me up at the airport.

"'Welcome, Cousin Valaida!'' is what Robert said to me and then tried to stick his tongue in my mouth when I offered him my cheek to kiss. When we got in their car, Marva pulled out one of those 'left-handed cigarettes' and lit it. I didn't have to make any excuses for not smoking because I've never been a smoker anyway.

"'When I look back on it, I have to laugh. They must've thought I was one of the great squares of the day. They took me to this beautiful apartment they had in that section of Chicago called Hyde Park and for the next two weeks it was a mad scene. That's the best description I can give.

"'They had two teenagers, a boy and girl, who were runnin' wild as monkeys. There was no established order for anything. Sometimes they ate at three in the morning. The rhythm of their lives was off. If you can possibly imagine what it would be like to live amongst a group of people who weren't sure of who they were, what they wanted, why they were doing what they were doing? Well, that would give you some indication of how things were. I didn't make too much of an effort to do anything with Cousin Marva and Brother Robert. That's what he asked me to call him. But I did make some effort to get through to the children.

"Where're you going, Aunt Valaida?"

"Over to the Museum of Science and Industry."

"What for?"

"C'mon with me 'n find out."

"'I didn't make an effort to get them to go with me to different places around the city, but would you believe? After five days they had accompanied me to the Museum of Science and Industry, the Art Institute—they were having a fantastic exhibit of the French Impressionists—the African-American Museum—these children hardly knew anything about their history—tours of historical sites in the city.

"'I was really astounded that I could go to a place where people had lived their whole lives and discover that they were almost totally ignorant of their surroundings. Cousin Marva and 'Brother' Robert both had good jobs and seemed to be fairly intelligent but the only thing they did, after work, was come home and smoke these 'left-handed cigarettes' and drink a lot of whiskey. They persuaded me to go to a party with them, the first weekend I was there, and the only thing they did that was different from what they usually did, was dance. Otherwise, they could've been at home.

"'It was my first trip away from home, from Augusta, and I didn't like it very much. I bent over backwards to be fair about what I was being exposed to and I still came to the same conclusions. The people were crude, selfish and ill mannered. They looked at me strangely because I said 'thank you' and 'please' so often. They didn't read very much and hardly knew what was going on in the world. What seemed to matter more than anything was to be 'up to date' which meant having the latest clothes, cars, jewelry and stuff like that.

"'They definitely did not have 'up to date' minds. I have to honestly say that I was quite happy to return to dear ol' Augusta. 'Brother' Robert made a goodbye rape attempt the night before my departure, which seemed almost appropriate, considering the barbaric nature of his lifestyle.'"

Chester paused to take a sip of water and to meet his wife's level gaze.

"Chester," she spoke in a low, even voice, "I find a great deal of similarity between this fictional character in your book and this real character lying beside you here in bed."

"You do?" he reacted with mock surprise.

157

"Yes, I do!"

He placed a marker in his notebook, closed it and placed it on the floor beside the bed and turned to wrap her in his arms. "Haven't you ever heard that fiction is sometimes closer to reality than truth is to itself?"

"O for heavens sake, Chester! Stop! You just made that up on the spur of the moment."

"It sounded good, didn't it?"

"Your little truisms always sound good, that's what makes you such a good writer."

They kissed, a long, tender kiss. After many trials and errors, they had become lovers, rather than people in love. He was always mindful of the fact that she had spent years with a man who hadn't been sensitive to her feelings and, although he never tried to make up for lost time, he constantly tried to let her know how much he loved her. The kiss wandered, became a gentle caress, a warmer kiss.

"Chester, do you know something?" she whispered.

"No, tell me."

"I think you're the most beautiful man I've ever known."

He felt a surge of feeling, a deep sense of love and passion.

"Valaida, you make me feel blessed when you say things like that."

Chapter 21

They got into the last twenty-five pages of "Simone" the following evening. Chester had decided to spice up the reading by preparing himself a shaker of martinis. Valaida propped herself up with two pillows, diet soda and peanuts nearby.

"Uhh, oh, it looks like the condemned writer had a stiff drink or two before the end, huh?" He winked at her, slightly tipsy from a couple taste-sips in the kitchen. "I like the way you put that." He retrieved the notebook, took a healthy sip of his martini, placed his glasses at the proper angle on his nose. "Now then, where did we leave off?"

"'Brother' Robert made an attempt to rape Simone the night before her departure."

"Ahh hahh, go on...

"'I returned to Augusta as though I were returning to a safe harbor. But gradually, I discovered that things were changing for me. My husband had been dead for a full year and more now and I became aware of what might be called 'plots' against me. A whole collection of men, some of them friends of my husband, made it their business to go out of their way to let me know that they had my best interests at heart, to let me know that I could call on them, if I needed anything. The only strings attached to what they were saying to me were my nightgown strings.

"'One of them went so far as to actually tell me that he had had a dream about his dick being in my pussy. I discovered a new Augusta. Women that I had never really had too much to do with in the first place suddenly discovered that I was a threat. I was really confused. I couldn't figure out why they felt threatened. When couples I knew came to the library or if I met them in the supermarket, the women would link their arms around their husbands as though they thought I was going to try to seduce them right on the spot.

"'I made the mistake of going to lunch with Mr. Hargraves, my supervisor down at the library. He wanted to talk with me about bringing more books on African-American history into the library and the nasty rumor got started that I was his mistress or some such thing.

"'Mr. Hargraves is white, of course, and that stimulated even more nasty talk. I was beginning to feel damned from every direction.

"'I wasn't interested in getting married again, but I can't say that I was enjoying my widowhood. This was not the kind of situation that would allow me to read a book about someone's life and lose myself in that character. The children were away at school most of the time and, so far as they were concerned, I was living a very fine life. I had a home, a decent job, money in the bank, good health. What more could I want? I wanted to break down a dozen times and tell them how miserable I was.

"'In some kind of strange way, I had managed to go

160

through years of a loveless marriage that produced three intelligent, sensible, loving individuals and now, at thirty-seven I was ready for love but I couldn't find it. It was being denied me for some reason. How can I explain it? I wanted a man's touch, but not just any man. And then, to be perfectly honest, there were times when I didn't feel the need to be close to anyone.

"'I think I must have acquired the reputation for being aloof, for being mysterious and all the other names that people have called me. Yes, I suppose I was aloof, I had to be, in order to protect myself.

"I made a once a week trip to the Gold Star dining room to have some of Sarah Robinson's fried catfish and there were times when I felt compelled to get a carry out dinner because I couldn't stand the way people looked at me. I guess we could say that I was a bit paranoid. I went back and forth to the library and performed my duties but my life was empty. I took me almost two years to realize how great a role Tom had played in my life. While he was alive my only connection with the outside world had been the library. The rest of my life had literally belonged to him. .

"'I had read every book in the library but, in a way, that made me a special kind of idiot. All of my knowledge was purely theoretical. I can't actually say what provoked the change in me, what collection of forces pushed me out. Perhaps there is something to the notion that if we go far enough around in a circle, we'll eventually wind up where we started.'"

Chester paused to sip his martini and take a reaction glance at his wife's face. She released a tight smile.

"Go on, Chester, read. The truth never hurt anybody."

He took another, longer sip before continuing.

"'I was sick of my empty life and I was determined to do something about it. I wanted a man and I was determined

161

to do something about that, too. Yes, I wanted a man. I wanted to have a man make love to me, stick his dick in me, fuck me. Do all of the things that I had read about in every erotic novel I'd ever read. But I was afraid and I knew whatever I did would have to be with a stranger.

"'There are two rumor mills in Augusta, in the South. There is the Black rumor mill and the white rumor mill. Some people say that there are so many rumors circulating in the Black rumor mill that the white one operates on its leakage.

"'In any case, the rumor mill put out the information that a new man had come to town and was staying at the Gold Star Hotel. He was first thought to be a con man or some kind of snake oil salesman. People said he had sneaky eyes and was reputed to be on the make for every female who came into the dining room. He sounded like the ideal man for me, I wanted a philanderer, not a husband.

"'It isn't difficult to get information about anything in Augusta, if you really want it. I found out that he usually came down into the dining room about five thirty a.m. or so and that he had discovered the Friday catfish dinner just like everyone else.

"'Suddenly, for the first time in my life, I became a designing woman. I was going to insinuate myself into this man's life and have sex with him. I was going to fuck him, to be crude about it. Mrs. Robinson was quite surprised, to say the least, when I suggested, when I strongly suggested that she seat me at the stranger's table. They all called him Mr. Richards to his face, but behind his back he was "the stranger." It wasn't difficult to single him out. It had something to do with the unusual shape of his eyes. If it hadn't been for his dark skin and kinky hair, you might think that he was Japanese.'"

Chester, also known by the nickname, "The Great Lawd Buddha" paused for another sip of his drink. Valaida stroked his arm absently, a warm smile on her mouth.

"'I wasn't certain how I was going to do it but I had resolved to end my involuntary celibacy by any means necessary, as the revolutionaries used to say. My plan was to sit across from him for the course of the dinner and then, at the end, scribble on a napkin—"your place or mine?" Or something like that.

"'Needless to say, I froze when the critical moment came. As a matter of fact, the crucial moment came and went a dozen times and, at the conclusion of the meal, I almost jumped up and ran. I felt like a calculating bitch, if you'll pardon the expression, and I had come into this innocent person' life (without his knowledge) with designs that he had no suspicions of. I had found, during the course of our dinner, that he wasn't the womanizer that the gossip had made him out to be. He struck me as an intelligent, decent person who was interested in the finer things of life.

"'I spent a week fantasizing about all of the things I could have talked to him about. And lo 'n behold! He popped up at the library, looking shy and a bit confused. Was this the woman-killer that they were talking about? He was beginning to wear his heart on his sleeve but I was too blind to see it. In my determination to have my celibacy come to an immediate end, I ignored his obvious interest in me. Sounds confusing, doesn't it? He had become interested in me, but I was oblivious to the fact because I was concentrating on my own agenda.

"'He took a bold step and asked that I should be seated at his table the next time I came into the dining room. Yes, I was surprised. I almost seemed as though my wishes were coming true without any effort on my part. We talked and he confessed that he was quite interested in me. I think that changed my mind around, from thinking like a mercenary to being pursued like a desired female. I was flattered.

"'He walked me home one evening and kissed me. I pretended to be outraged. A little game I developed that I became the master of. My desire to simply do something lascivious gave way to another kind of urge. I felt the urge to have this man in my life, I wanted to be a part of his life.

"'I had strong suspicion that he simply wanted to have his way with me and that was all. I didn't want that. Yes, of course, I said that that's what I wanted in the beginning, but then I changed. That's a woman's prerogative, isn't it? The more we got to know about each other, the more interested I became in him, but, of course, I didn't tell him that.

"'He had been everywhere and done everything and I had only been to Chicago. I had to admit that I had serious doubts about us, about us being together. I know, it all sounds contradictory. But that is a woman's prerogative, isn't it?

"'When he asked me to marry, after months of trying to convince me that we should go to bed together, without the burden of marriage, I almost refused him. I mean, here we were, at a point that I had been almost fantasizing about and it was happening. I held out for as long as I could, and then, in the autumn (naturally) of 1988, we became man and wife.

"'I started this journal the day after we were married. I know that it would never mean anything to the public, this basically dull life of a woman who made no great efforts to change the world, to influence public opinion, or to govern her own life. Maybe, if it has any message to offer, that message might be, don't surrender.'"

Chester took a long swig from his glass, a bit puffed up about his accomplishment.

"That it?" Valaida asked gently.

"That's it," he replied.

"Chester, what do you propose to do with this particular

164

work?''

"Well, Franklin House is committed to publishing it, number one...you have any objection?''

"Why should I have objections? Because you fused bits and pieces of things you know about me and twisted them around to fit the framework of someone called Simone?''

"Well?''

They both laughed. "No, Mr. Simmons, I don't feel outraged about your clever manipulations. Frankly, I feel somewhat bored.''

"Bored?''

"Will you hate me if I'm terribly critical?''

"You know how thick my skin is.''

"Well, as a librarian, one of the things I've fought against for years, is having books like 'Simone' on our reading list.''

"But, why honey? People love to read complex character studies of ordinary people. Remember the Robert Altman movie, *Ordinary People*?''

"I'd rather read a complex character study of a complex character.''

"So, you're saying that 'Simone doesn't work for you?''

"I'm afraid I have to say yes to that.''

"Can you give me a specific reason?''

Valaida Simmons stared at the ceiling for a few beats. "I think it has too much of me in it, and I'm not interesting enough to carry a novel. I don't know who the early role model was in your novel...''

"I didn't have a role model, that's why I latched onto you.''

"Well, in my opinion, you made a mistake.''

A half hour later, snuggled next to each other in the dark, he reviewed "Simone" and reluctantly agreed with her. "Valaida, you sleep, baby?''

"No, why?''

"I was just thinking, won't it be something if this mediocre novel becomes a best seller?"

"It happens all the time, sweetheart, it happens all the time."

He hugged her closer to him. What a lucky bastard I am. How often does a man wind up with a beautiful woman who is honest enough to tell her man the truth, no matter what the price?

Chapter 22

"Simone" did not become a best seller, but it sold well, because of the aggressive advertising campaign that Franklin House waged on its behalf. Chester L. Simmons gradually settled into the life of Augusta's Black intellectual community. He tried to prevent it from happening by confessing that he had once served fifteen years for a murder. But his confession was brushed aside by reality. "Chester, all of us have done something wrong at some point. We can't dwell on that."

One evening, at a community meeting to discuss the lack of knowledge that black students at the local, prestigious small college had of African and African-American geopolitics, under the influence of his wife's urgings, Chester stood up and orated himself into a teaching post.

The class was labeled Black Geopolitics by the school administration and re-labeled African Geopolitics by the instructor, Mr. Simmons. He was forced to explain the reason to the Board of Trustees of Daniel Benson College.

"Gentlemen, you must understand by now that semantical racial abuses in the Western World and, of course, elsewhere, automatically relegate the adjective *blacks* to any area that concerns Africans. I am totally rejecting the adjective for use in describing my course because it will not be dealing with Black world politics, but with African world politics.

"Black world politics would automatically ghetto-ize what I intend to bring to these young people, *African* would not."

The three whites on the board argued almost as viciously as one of the Blacks on the Board for the use of Black, rather than African. "Mr. Simmons, with all due respect, sir, we are not Africans, we are Black Americans."

"I beg to differ with you, Mr. Bumfellow, we are African people in America, which makes us African-Americans, not Blacks, or Black Americans."

"But, Mr. Simmons . . ."

"I know, the media and a lot of mistaken African-Americans have always called themselves "Black". It's time we corrected that distortion. If anyone in this room should happen to hear me refer to myself or anyone else of African descent as a Black, then please don't hesitate to correct me.

"As you all know, there is no place on the planet called Blackland, the place where Blacks come from, but there is an Africa and it is no longer mistakenly called 'the dark continent'."

After two hours of Chester L. Simmons' hard nosed arguments, all seven members of the Board more or less conceded. "Well, Mr. Simmons, I have to say that I don't totally agree with you . . ."

"I'm not after total consensus, Mr. Porges. I'm after the most logical title for the course I'll be teaching. Or I won't be teaching, depending on this Board's decision." The decision to hire him was provoked by a demonstration of

168

students at Daniel Benson College.

"We want Afri-can Geo-poli-tics! We want Afri-can Geo-poli-tics! We want Afric-can Geo-poli-tics!"

It was the first time in Benson College history that the students had ever demanded anything. And they got what they wanted. Chester L. Simmons became a college instructor. His credentials consisted of an ability to read, write and say exactly what he felt like saying. He had days, facing thirty freshly washed faces (two of them white), when he felt as though he were back in the joint, trying to make the neophyte cons understand what prison really meant.

"What you must be completely clear about is why you're here. If you're here to get a degree, then you're in the wrong class. No degrees are granted here. I'm not even going to suggest that I will offer you the raw material to get a degree. A degree, as it must be presently defined, is simply that, a de-gree. It is not something that will allow you to add to it because it is a de-gree, and once you get it, you can get another one more easily but I guarantee you this...you won't know anymore. What I'm offering you is a class of 'inner-cation', which means that your ability to earn a degree will be limited by the amount of bullshit you'll be able to tolerate.

"If my course in 'inner-cation' makes enough of an impact on you, many of you will drop out of school and become fools for life. I don't want to suggest that 'fools for life' is equivalent to being stupid, dense, disoriented, crazed by the suns of academia or any such thing. 'fools for life' will take you into Reality, which is where academic bullshit comes to a screechin' halt."

African Geopolitics became one of the most successful non-academic courses taught at Daniel Benson College. And Brother Chester L. Simmons (he insisted that the College brochure list him as "Brother") became one of the most popular and sought after people in town.

169

"Well, Mr. Simmons, it seems that you've really made your mark. Here is an invitation to address the Scottish Club."

"What's that?"

"The Scottish Club? The Scottish Club is a group of the most influential Black, Uhhh. . . African-Americans in town. They are the ones who can say 'yea' or 'nay' and make changes happen."

"Why do they call themselves 'The Scottish Club?'"

"I think it has something to do with having meetings in something called The Scottish Club?"

"Chester, you'll have to talk to them about that. I don't have the slightest notion."

After three X-rated speeches to The Scottish Club, Chester was elected vice-president. "As I look around me here, at all the Scotts, I am reminded of the old German proverb that a Croatian diplomat once told to a Swiss banker in Rome, on the eve of that greatest of all Scottish holidays, Malcolm X Day." His sarcasm brought him to the attention of the First World Party's regional chairman.

"Mr. Simmons, we want you to be our candidate for Mayor of this town." He resisted the invitation to run for office until Mrs. Simmons gave him one of her no-nonsense lectures. "Chester, let's face it, you talk about the bad situation most African-Americans find themselves in, politically because they don't participate in the political process and now you're saying that you won't participate? And you're teaching a course entitled 'African Geopolitics'? C'mon, honey, let's shit or get off the pot."

The campaign was relatively gentle, in comparison to the usual dirt and grit of most big city political races, and Chester L. Simmons became the mayor of Augusta, Georgia. He was humbled by the honor.

"Valaida, do you have any idea what this really means

to me? Here I am, a nobody . . .''

''Chester, you were never a 'nobody'.''

''Well, you know what I means? I come from almost nothing and here I am, the Mayor of the city I live in.''

''Let's slip all the post election rhetoric and see if you really are the right person for the job.''

Chapter 23

Mayor Simmons became one of the movers and shakers in the state's political set up. He quietly, but efficiently turned Augusta into the closest example of a model city that many people had ever seen.

"Mr. Mayor, we are impressed by the fact that you seem to have eradicated two of the most cancerous elements on the American scene: racism and the drug problem. Can you explain to our viewers how this was accomplished?"

"Well, I could sit here and offer you a bunch of rhetoric, but I won't. The problems of racism and drug abuse still exist in Augusta, but I think what we've done is scale them down to almost nil."

"And I'm asking you, how was it done?"

"It's being done by all means necessary."

Chester L. Simmons, aka The Great Lawd Buddha to a close collection of hip people, writer, raconteur, gourmet chef, linguist, ex-convict, was reelected to office twice, defeating all challengers.

"Valaida, you know something?"

"What?"

"I think we need to make a move, change our perspective. I'm beginning to feel that I'm not being challenged hard enough by life."

Valaida Hurston-Simmons slowly lowered her latest book, "The Good Life", and stared into his face, question marks hooking her eyebrows up. "And just what do you have in mind that would be more challenging?"

"Well, the idea of leaving here and going to Africa has been brewing in my head for a while."

"Africa?"

"Yeahhh, South Africa, Azania, to be exact. I think that would offer a few challenges. What do you think?"

"When do you want to leave?"

"Ohhh, I was think about the end of this term in office, the end of this year."

"Sounds like a winner to me, Chester, I'll start getting our passports and stuff in order."

He watched her return to reading his latest book, a clearly critical frown wrinkling her aristocratic forehead.

God, what a beautiful woman to share this beautiful life with. If I had known it was going to be this sweet I would've gotten off into it sooner.

Epilogue 1

Chester Simmons stared at his wife's profile, trying to remember a poem he had once read in praise of the beauty of African women.

"What're you thinking about, Chester?"

He could feel the gleam in her eyes behind the big chic sunglasses. "Oh, this 'n that. About what it'll be like to be in Spain with you."

They both turned to stare over the railing at the deep blue-green Atlantic. It was her idea to sail to Europe on a luxury freighter. "I got the idea from reading all those lies you wrote about traveling places on ships 'n what not." They seemed to be almost ideally suited to each other, looking out for each others backs, covering up the places where one or the other left blanks.

A fifteen day trip across the Atlantic, time to probe each others psyches again.

"Chester, why do you get so angry whenever I mention

my dead husband's name?''

"I don't get angry. I just don't see the point in talking about a dead man.''

She fought the urge to be jealous of his previous affairs with other women.

"Valaida, if I had known you were going to trip out about this, I wouldn't have mentioned the subject.'' Valaida was a gorgeous experience for Chester. Whenever he felt had a handle on her personality, she would do a change up on him, creating an infinitely interesting personality.

They turned toward each other to exchange sad smiles, thinking the same sad thought. "You know something, baby, there are times when I really feel what our ancestors felt being brought across this ocean.''

"I know. I feel that, too.''

The luxury freighter was populated by hard working Spanish men, a reclusive group of passengers and only a few recreational distractions. Chester and Valaida spent hours sitting in deck chairs, reading, talking or simply staring out at the blue horizon. "Chester, how do you think this world is going to come to an end?''

"I already told you, it came to an end a few million light years ago. We're living in the past right now.''

"What makes you say that?''

"Look at it logically. There is no way a world like ours could've continued: the pollution, the hatred, the wars, the horror of human inhumanity. How could an Earth have continued after the water supply had been poisoned? The food sources contaminated? The sex-love lives of the people destroyed and it wasn't the usual bad guys like America and Japan that did it either. We all had a hand in destroying ourselves.''

"Hmmm . . . I'll have to think on that one.''

They were making heavy afternoon love when the ship

anchored at Valencia.

"Oh, Chester, come look. How beautiful!"

Yes, how beautiful. He sprawled on the narrow bed they had slept on, took naps on, make love on for almost three weeks and stared at Valaida's naked back. Yes, how beautiful.

They strolled on to shore a few hours later, feeling confident and adventurous. Chester's mind pulsated with thoughts of his last visit to this city. El Encanto was Valencia. The broasted chickens, slowly whirling on open spits, the hesitant voice of a sleepy flamenco singer.

He picked an expensive hotel for them to spend their first weekend in Spain. "We'll hang out in Valencia for a couple days, give you a change to get your land legs back."

"Whatever you say, sweetheart." She humored him outrageously, content to enjoy his program. Chester felt like a millionaire. He had thousands of dollars to spend, a beautiful woman at his side and six months to cope with an adventurous itinerary.

"Okay, here's what we're gonna do. We'll do Spain for a couple weeks, check Madrid out, stroll the boulevards, that kind of thing. Then, we'll drop down the southeast coast to Gibraltar and cross over to Africa." They had put together a slow, non-tourist type travel agenda. "We don't want to feel rushed about anything. We get to some place we like, we'll just hang in there until we get tired of it."

"And if we get to someplace we don't like we'll leave immediately."

"That's right!"

Europe meant Spain; Africa was going to be the real trip. Africa meant Casablanca, Morocco, Mauritania, Senegal, Guinea, Liberia, Ivory Coast, Ghana, Togo, Benin, Nigeria, Cameroon, Gabon, Congo, Angola, Namibia and on into the recently independent South African country of Azania.

176

"Chester, don't you think we have a few too many places on this list?"

"We'll soon find out, won't we?"

Valaida was a delightful traveling companion. Her sense of humor and efficiency made the most complicated problems seem simple. He picked the spots and she made all the rest of it happen.

Valencia laid an emotional weight on him, he couldn't get El Encanto out of his mind. On their last evening in town he took her on an El Encanto style tour of Valencia. The names of the joints they toured were different, but the people seemed to be the same.

"This guy drank cognac like water. We sat up in here, right at this table as a matter of fact, many nights, drinking cognac."

"What else did you all do?"

"Not too much of anything else, take my word for it."

They decided not to go to Madrid, but rather to continue down the coast to Alicante.

"Fina" was dead. He wasn't surprised. But his friend, the cab driver, Zurriaga, was alive and overwhelmed to see him again. "You coming back, I don' believe! I don' believe!"

Chester's admiration for Valaida grew each day. She was an "ol' fashioned Southern belle" who had never fallen into a helpless mode, never surrendered to mental laziness and was superbly gracious. "Chester, you never told me you had such wonderful friends."

Finally, like bird's flying a migratory pattern, it was time to move on. They decided to rent a car and drive south to Gibraltar. "Nothing like driving through a country to get the feel of it."

"Why don't we send our large bags ahead and hike?"

"Uhhh, Valaida, honey. We want to get a feel for the

177

country, not the whole emotion. You know what I mean?''

They drove through the dry Spanish plains at midnight, feeling deliciously wicked as they sipped excellent Spanish sherries. ''I would never do this in the States.''

''Why not?''

''They'd arrest me.''

''They would arrest you here too, wouldn't they? If we got caught.''

''I think we ought to put the cork back in and put the bottle in the boot. We can have the rest for lunch. Or with our Siesta.'' The Siesta was a lovely custom that they turned into an almost daily two hour love session. In Cartagena, they rented an apartment in a 16th century castle and sprawled on top of the huge royal bed, naked, to watch the sun slowly sink like a lollipop being swallowed by a giant mouth.

In Almeria, they swam in the Mediterranean, lunched on fresh shrimp and beer and fell asleep in each others arms. The Spanish seemed to see them as good omens going through their towns, through their lives. ''Chester, don't you think it's ironic that the Spanish, who were first degree slave traders, should be so gracious?''

''Yeahhh, I guess it is kind of ironic in a way, but what you have to remember is that the Spanish, deep down, always looked at slavetrading as an economics number. They used the Church to justify their stuff, but I don't think anybody really went for it. The difference, I think, had to do with how devious the Church was and is. The Church was and is like a big corporation. It has a lot of branches and covers a lot of ground. The Protestants used their church to prove that African people were inferior heathens and then they tried to force themselves to believe it. That gave them the proper amount of guilt complex whenever they raped African, Indian and Asian women. The Catholics, Spanish and Portuguese, didn't buy into that kind of thinking. If they had, we wouldn't have a Mexico or a Brazil, racially speaking."

They went to see the grandsons of Antonio Ordonez and Luis Dominguin fight mano a mano in Malaga. Chester gave her the short form of what the bullfight was all about. "It's a bloody ritual, Valaida. It's like what the Religion is for African people all over the world. The bullfight pre-dates the Catholic Church and, despite the grumbling we hear from time to time, it's probably going to be here after the Church is gone."

"A bloody ritual?"

"Yep, that's what it is. A man goes into the arena armed with a cape and a sword and if he does his job right, a man-symbol, the bull, will be killed. El Encanto saw the bullfighter as a female symbol, who lures the male symbol with his red cloth. Others see him as a priest who is simply serving the people, doing something that they are afraid to do. The aesthetics of the corrida are very African in many ways. There is this big involvement with the color, rhythm and deep feeling. And the sacrifice, don't forget the sacrifice. In every area of our life, if we want to get something, we have to give up something."

Chano Ordonez and Mongo Dominguin fought three bulls each, alternating, brilliantly. It took Chester many miles to explain what had happened. Valaida felt that she had been present at a great ceremony. "You know I really thought you were putting me on a bit when you talked about the bullfighters as priests. But I could see it clearly midway in the fight, when they came out to dedicate the bull. Remember when the first man. . .?"

"Chano Ordonez, the grandson of Antonio Ordonez."

"Yes, that one, When he stood in the center of the ring and turned to dedicate the first bull to us. I felt like crying. And I would never have been able to tell you why."

"I felt that way, too. Strange, isn't it, that a man in a bright colored pair of leotards, a cute little bolero jacket and a cape could make you feel that kind of emotion."

The fight was one of those historical dinosaurs, two grandsons of two of the most honored figures in the taurine world had come to the city of Malaga to honor the memory of their grandfathers. And they had done exactly that. The aficion remembers the event as a positive demonstration of what the corrida can be when the participants are brave, skillful and honorable.

"You have to understand, honor plays a big role in the bullfight. The best, like the two men we saw, have placed themselves beyond tricks, beyond movie-star-neon-lights-flashing bullfighting. They were truly honorable men."

They made a visit to the Gypsy caves above Jerez de la Frontera to hear a flamenco singer named 'Fina'.

"Honey, I've told you all about my ex-landlady. If there is anybody else in the world named 'Fina' singing flamenco, we have to go see her." Strangely, they both felt that there were no tourists other than the two of them in the Gypsy cave. "Maybe it's got something to do with how late it is. How many tourists get out to see or hear something at two a.m.?" The Gypsies treated them with cordial reserve, no hustle, no games, no attempts to force them to sing along or clap along with the complex rhythms and melodies. The music began with the strumming of a single guitar and gradually moved upward and beyond. Ana Albaicin 'Fina' took one step away from the group and began to improvise siginyas.

"Chester," Valaida whispered at one point, "is this the blues or is this the blues?"

"You got it right, baby, this is the Spanish Gypsy version."

The sun was slowly moving up from the horizon as they walked out of the cave. Chester gave the owner of the cave a hundred dollar bill and a smile. Valaida's expression was solemn. "What's the problem, baby?"

"No problem, exactly. I was just thinking about how isolated most African-Americans are. I wonder how many of our people have ever listened to this music?"

"Well, you know how it is, flamenco, like jazz, like Tibetan temple music and a few other types of esoteric music, just ain't for everybody."

"I guess you're right. Chester.?"

"Yeah, baby . . ."

"Let's go to the hotel, I feel drained."

"Me, too." They strolled down the hillside like zombies, their emotions trapped in the cave behind them. Fina's voice echoing in the back of their minds. Two days later they were crossing the Straits of Gibraltar to Africa. Tangier had all the romantic feeling of a Tiajuana whorehouse. "We're going to move out of here sharply."

"I can see what happens when tourism becomes a hustle."

A rented 1985 VW Bug saved them from the hordes of vendors and beggars who surrounded them whenever they walked through the streets. "First stop, Casablanca . . ."

Casablanca was a milder version of Tangier. "Chester, you know something? I don't have a strong sense of being in Africa yet. In some ways Augusta, Georgia feels more African than this place."

"I know what you mean. I've always had mixed feelings about Morocco, ever since their king allowed that filthy rich publisher to throw a multi-million dollar birthday party in his country. Can you imagine the degree of insensitivity a person would have to have in order to put on a wasteful show like that? Next door to where thousands of people are either starving or don't have enough to eat from day to day?"

They decided to play out a little fantasy in Casablanca. "Good afternoon, you have reservation for Mr. and Mrs.

Victor Laslo?'' The desk clear, an evil looking Frenchman with a Frankenstein scar on the left cheek, didn't even blink as he rifled through his files.

"Sorry, sir, nothing for Victor Lazlo."

"How about Mr. and Mrs. Chester Simmons?" the desk clerk's eyelashes flickered a couple times but he asked no questions about why a Black man named Simmons should be asking about reservations for Lazlo. Valaida sprawled across the generous bed, laughing as Chester played the spy role, checking the lamps for hidden mikes, peeking around the corner of the curtain for suspected enemies on the corner. "I don't care how far you take this, just so long as you don't start calling me Ilse."

Epilogue 2

Rick's Cafe Americain proved to have irresistible drawing power. "Who knows? We might run across Bogart and Bergman in here." Rick's Cafe Americain was a fair duplication of the movie saloon, except that the piano was replaced by a five piece jazz quintet. "Table for two, sir?"

"Yes, you have a reserved table for Victor Lazlo?"

"I'm afraid not, sir."

"No problem, we'll take that table over there by the wall."

"Chester, you're worse than an incorrigible little boy. Why do you keep playing this little in-joke out on these people?"

Just for kicks, baby, just for kicks. I just want to see who remembers the movie?"

"More likely than not, they've never heard of it." They ordered glasses of white wine and people watched Chester playing out a stream of character sketches for Valaida.

"Valaida, check him out, that big round toad over there.

If that ain't a living impersonation of Sydney Greenstreet, I'll eat my hat.''

"Hmmm, he's big enough to be somebody." They both had to giggle at the nervous Peter Lorre who seemed capable, at any moment, of screeching, "Rick, Rick! Save me! Don't let them take me, please! Rick! Rick!"

The piano player with the jazz quartet didn't resemble Dooley Wilson and the quintet had only the vaguest idea of what real jazz sounded like.

Casablanca, with all of its cinematic and political history, was a bust. "Maybe we expected too much from the place."

"Yeahhh, maybe you got a point there, baby. I mean, were never shown this side of Casablanca in the movie, the flyspecks and the bullshit. One thing we do know is that there is a lot of corruption going, lots."

The desk clerk "overestimated" their bill by a fourth and the policeman who stopped Chester from driving the wrong way on a one way street gratefully accepted a ten dollar gratuity. They decided not to try to drive through Western Sahara ("might run into a little left over civil war or something") and Mauritania, but took a local airline from Casablanca to Dakar.

In the taxi from the airport to the Hotel Dakar, they turned to each other and nodded in silent agreement. This is where we come from. The streets literally throbbed with activity. People selling and buying, bustling from place to place, pausing to sip coffee in French style cafes. It was West Africa with a slight French tinge.

"Woww! Doesn't it blow your mind to have man that black open his mouth and start speaking French, of all things?"

"Well, look at us, speaking English. Just goes to show you that you can't tell the book by its cover."

"Whatever is that supposed to mean."

They settled into the scene. They went to the swank places

and the low dives. "Always go to where the real people go, that way you'll always know what the real deal is." They had become friendly with a number of people, who offered them all kinds of advice. One of them, a man named Mamadou, who always seemed to be around when they wanted know where the best restaurant was, or how to get to the National Museum. Or whatever.

"You must go to Casamance, to the south where I come from, to the real Senegal." After a week Chester decided to take him up on his advice.

"Mamadou, how much would you charge us to drive south and be our guide for a few days?" They agreed on a price and two days later they were heading south in Mamadou's ancient Citroen.

"One goes slowly in this vehicle, but one always arrives safely." They had to agree with Mamadou about a number of things. Yes, the Citroen was slow and Casamance was the real Senegal. The people seemed leaner, darker, more serious. The land was drier and the villages more widely dispersed.

"With your permission, I will take you to stay with my family. My father is an important man in this area." The Diop family opened up like a flower to receive them. The women took Valaida off to show her how to fix the gele properly, for a woman of her age and obvious social standing. The men took Chester to see their newly constructed mosque. He wasn't invited to go inside and didn't ask for the privilege. He followed Mamadou's father, a man who could have been an ancient pharoah, around the small mud and brick structure with the large cupola, thinking. God, what happened to my African brothers? How could they have allowed themselves to follow every religion that was thrown in their faces? We didn't have any choice in America, but what made them give up here, at home? He didn't find the submission to Islam difficult to understand. The Arabicized invaders came with swords and offered the people one choice, submit or die. The submission had been so complete that ninety percent of the people accepted Islam as though it had always been a part of their religious background, even when they blended some of their indigenous religious practices with it.

He heard the drums before the small boy trotted up to the senior Diop to whisper something.

Mamadou translated. "M'sieur Simmons, the people of the village have invited you to a dance in your honor." They walked through the heart of the village to the foot of a huge tree. Valaida was already there, seated in the middle of group of women. She sprinkled her fingers at him in a shy wave. He did a double take. She was wearing one of the more conservative gowns that she had purchased in Dakar and, if she had been a few shades darker, would have been just another woman of the village.

The dance was beginning. It was a clear, lean performance of movements that had obviously been shaped and honed for many years.

Chester felt frustrated about being seated so far away from Valaida, he felt the urge to defy tradition, but decided against it. He didn't want to disgrace Mamadou. They exchanged meaningful glances at different times during the afternoon. Chester was fascinated by the drums. During the first break in the playing, singing and dancing he questioned his guide-friend, "Mamadou, tell me something about the drums, what are they called?"

"I know very little of these drums, M'sieur Simmons, maybe my father . . .?"

The elder listened patiently to Chester's questions as they were being translated and, at the end of the fourth question, stroked his Mandarin spade beard and sent for the elder drummer. Chester suddenly felt uneasy, as though he had interrupted the flow of events just to have his curiosity satisfied. Mamadou put him at ease. "My father says it takes a wise man to know when questions should be asked." The elder drummer, a wizen little man with eyes like burning coals, squatted in front of the assembled group and waited for the questions to be translated. The assembled villagers seemed to be as curious as Chester and Valaida. The trio of drums were very old, the drummer explained. The whole set were called Kutero. The baby drum was called N'dingo, the middle drum was Kutero Ba, the father and the solo drum was called Sabaro, and it possessed male and female energy.

"Are the drums always played as a trio?"

"Yes."

"Why are they played with a stick in one hand?"

"Because that's the way the Kutero is always played."

It seemed, without actually doing it, that the elder drummer had closed off the questions. He stood slowly, bowed slightly to the senior Mamadou and went back to the drums. Chester flashed eye signals to Valaida, as though to say, it's deep, ain't it? She returned his signals with an affirmative nod, yes, yes it is. He felt something holy about the drums, this trio of bucket-sized drums, the skins pegged down, played with a palm and a stick. The intricacy of the playing bewildered him. The smallest drum carried one rhythm the middle drum, Ba, played another rhythm and the lead drum was playing above and beyond the other two. They only rhythmic connection he could make was the Bata drums, the sacred drums of the Yoruba. Maybe these are the same thing. I'll have to do a little research.

The dances that accompanied the drums were reflections of the diverse rhythms, clear, simple but immensely complex. Valaida felt fatigued after an hour of watching the dancers. They seemed to bankrupt themselves with each movement and yet they carried on. The shimmering heat, the effervescent motions of the dancers, the precise strokes of the drummers, the singing of the villagers made Chester feel as though he were a part of something ancient.

This is *our* tradition, not neon lights, shiny new cars, houses piled up like layers, crazy ideas, warped thinking, Westernized bullshit. This is our tradition.

The dance in their honor came to a natural conclusion, not an ending. The natural conclusion led them to feel that there was more to come, on another day, at another time. The villager's gathered around them, clapping and singing. Mamadou translated, They are saying, "Welcome to our village, brother and sister, be at ease, this is our home, no one will harm you here. Welcome."

Hours later, after a delicious dinner of rice, chicken, peanut sauce and greens, Chester and Valaida sat on the porch of the guest house, staring up at the stars. "Chester, this is so beautiful." He nodded in agreement, there was nothing to say. The silence of the night was a framework for thousands of unfamiliar sounds. The sky seemed to be filled with billions of stars, so close that they could reach up and pluck them out of the air. *Be at ease, this is your home, no one will harm you here, welcome.* They had to leave three days later because of Mamadou.

"Forgive me my friends, but I must return to my employment."

"Employment? What employment?"

"I am the assistant manager of the Hotel Dakar."

They shared a laugh. They had never really known what he was or what he did. He just always seemed to be available and helpful. Chester slipped Mamadou's father a hundred dollar bill and felt that he was almost cheating the man for the hospitality they had been given. "M'sieur Simmons, you didn't have to do that. My father loves to have visitors . . ."

"I know I didn't have to do it, Mamadou, but I wanted to."

188

The clear beautiful tones of the Kutero drums echoed in their ears as they drove back to Dakar. Valaida cried. "Those were some really beautiful people, Chester, really beautiful. Mamadou?"

"Yes, Madame...?"

"Thank you for taking us to the real Senegal."

"It was my pleasure, Madame, it was my pleasure."

Epilogue 3

In some extraordinary way word was out that Mr. and Mrs. Chester Simmons were touring the western edge of the continent. They received an invitation to attend the inauguration of the mayor of Monrovia, Liberia. "Wowww! This sorta makes us celebrities or something, doesn't it?"

"Make you feel that way, doesn't it?"

They made a hard decision to fly over Guinea-Bissau, Guinea and Sierra Leone. They felt that they had stepped back a few years in American time when they arrived in Monrovia. They knew the history of Liberia and how the original colonists and had raped the worst of their former owners.

"Mr. and Mizz Simmons, my name is George W. Carter, Mayor Lincoln's personal representative. I've been instructed to take you to State House and to see that you are comfortable. His honor will be receiving guests tomorrow evening and you and Mrs. Simmons are invited, of course.

They felt pleased to be so cordially received but there was something in the air, they could sense it as they were being driven to State House.

"Mr. Simmons, I've had the pleasure of reading several of your works. I wonder if I could bring a couple of them over for your autograph?"

"Yes, Mr. Carter, I'd be more than happy to autograph your books."

Valaida and Chester, turned into their special radar system, took note of the truck loads of armed soldiers scurrying around, the hostile expressions of the few people on the streets. "Uhh, Mr. Carter? Why are there so many soldiers rushing around town?" Mr. Carter flexed his neck muscles uncomfortably a couple times.

"Soldiers rushing around, Mrs. Simmons? Oh, they are preparing for Mr. Lincoln's inauguration on Sunday." Chester winked at his wife. Bullshit happening here.

State House could've been the facade of an American pre-Civil War plantation house, complete with uniformed servants. The glaring difference was the presence of soldiers with automatic weapons strategically arranged about the premises. Mr. Carter made a suave departure after making certain that their baggage was taken in.

"Mr. and Mrs. Simmons, welcome to Liberia. If there is anything you need, please see Mr. Jenkins here. He will do everything to make your stay as enjoyable as possible. His honor will be having a small, rather informal dinner later this evening. Maybe you'd like to come?"

"Thank you, give us time to think about it. It's pretty hot and we've had a long trip."

Mr. Carter's eyes bulged as he repeated, gritting the words out, "Maybe you'd like to come?"

Valaida chilled out the hostility brightly, "We'll be there."

Carter bowed out, leaving the Simmones to puzzle out what

they had blundered into. The door was barely closed before they started talking to each other.

"O my God! Chester, we've stumbled into a damned revolution or something. Why didn't someone warn us?"

"It might not be what it looks like. Let's give it a chance."

"It looks like a revolution or some kind of *coup* is in the works. I've read a lot about stuff like this. I wouldn't even know which side to be on if it were happening."

"I think you're right. We have to get out of here, but we probably won't be able to leave before Sunday. That's three days away. We accepted on invitation, right?"

The sudden chatter of gunfire made them duck into each other's arms. They huddled under one of the large tables in their room. "Valaida, ain't this a bitch!? We had to come halfway around the world to get caught in some bullshit like this!"

Valaida, always cool and calm, pursed her lips. It was all she had to say. After a few minutes of close listening they could tell that the gunfire was coming from a distance. They looked sheepishly at each other, bunched up under the table, and laughed at themselves. "Well, one thing is certain, no one is going to be able to sneak up on us." They crawled from under the table and began to do some logical brainstorming.

"Chester, I don't quite know what the deal is, but I think we had better get the hell out of this place."

"I think you're right."

The sound of automatic weapons was spliced with an occasional thud. "Sounds like mortar bombardment."

Mr. Jenkins knocked three hours later to inform them that the dinner hour was at five p.m. sharp.

"Uhh, Mr. Jenkins, we've been hearing a lot of automatic weapons being fire over the last few hours and what sounds like mortars. What's happening?"

Mr. Jenkins, obviously a snob's snob from way back, tilted his broad nose up as he answered. "It's nothing, suh, just a bunch of unruly niggers lettin' off steam."

They stared at him in disbelief. An African man in Liberia calling other Africans niggers? Oh well, the history of Liberia could explain a lot of what that was about.

"Thank you, Mr. Jenkins," Valaida answered graciously and gently closed the door in his face. "What do you make of it, baby?"

"I'd suggest we make it, out of here."

"Let's do that, right after dinner. I'm hungry." She grabbed him in a playful bear hug. "Chester Simmons! You are too much, you know that?"

"I know, I know."

They hugged and kissed, glad to be in each others arms.

The 'small, informal dinner' consisted of thirty people, seated around a huge table. Chester felt ill at ease with the stuffed shirts fanned out around the table, and most of all with Sir Benjamin Lincoln, the Mayor-elect of Monrovia. "Valaida," he whispered, "you ever been around this many pootbutts at one time?"

"Not since my days at St. Simon's Girl's School."

The thirty dinner guests were an elite selection of Liberians, upper crust American diplomatic types, a few Englishmen and several Lebanese entrepreneurs. It was quite obvious that the 'ordinary' Liberian hadn't been invited. The gunfire they had heard earlier was intermittent now, but seemed to be closer.

"We've got to get some information, find out what's happening."

"You got that right. You see what you can get from your side, I'll go the other way."

Valaida turned to the young Liberian diplomat at her right and flashed a winning, seductive smile. Chester turned to his left and encountered a stoic face of a red-faced English man.

"Pardon, how do you do? May name is Mrs. Valaida Simmons, and your name is...?"

"Gabriel Jones, of the Liberian diplomatic service."

"Ahhem, Mr. Jones, what is that noise we hear from time to time?"

"Uhh, what noise, m'am?"

"Those gunshots and those thuds, like bombs falling?"

The Liberian glanced around nervously. "Oh, it is nothing, I assure you. Just a few people letting off steam."

"I see, said the blind man."

"Beg your pardon?"

"Oh nothing. Just talking to myself."

She turned to Chester and signalled, nothing here. He took the cue and started in on the Englishman. "We haven't been introduced. My name is Chester Simmons."

"Yes, of course. Reginald Cornfog here." Chester had to consciously prevent himself from laughing in the man's face. Cornfog? Cornfog. You look like a cornfog, too. "Mr. Cornfog, pleased to meet you. Say, look, what's the gunfire we hear all about?"

The Englishman took a sip of his Mouton Cadet, took a surreptitious look around the table and begin to speak out of the corner of his mouth like a San Quentin inmate. "What you heah, Mr. Simmons, is the sound of the opposition forces closing in."

"Opposition forces? I don't understand?"

"Let me explain to you briefly what the situation is."

"Please do."

"Mr. Lincoln, the chap over there who recently won the city by fraudulent means, belongs to the Republican party. He had most of the leaders of the Independent party jailed when it appeared that his bid to become Mayor for the third time was in jeopardy. The Independent Party members are now on the edge of the city, threatening to take over by force of arms and that, in brief, is where the matter stands.''

"Doesn't it seem strange that Mr. Lincoln is so calm, giving dinner parties and stuff.''

"Well, he couldn't really duck his head under the table and hide, now could he?''

"You really think the Independent forces can take over, and if they do, what'll happen?''

"Well, I suspect that His Honor the Mayor will be executed and most of his staff given long prison sentences. They've already assassinated Mr. Lincoln's right hand man, this afternoon.''

"His right hand man?''

"A chap named Carter.''

"George Carter?''

"Yes, of course, you must know him. He welcomed you today, didn't he?''

"Yes, he did. You seem to know a lot, Mr. Cornfog. What's all this mean to you?''

Cornfog picked a speck of dirt from under his immaculate fingernails and smiled like a cat.

"I deal in arms, Mr. Simmons, there's a good deal in it for me.''

Chester felt nauseated by the man's smug arrogance. He was going to benefit from somebody's death, no matter where it took place. "That's interesting. Excuse me." He swirled around to Valaida and whispered, "You're right to the bone. There is a *coup* about to come off here and we could get caught in the middle. I just got the word from this vulture to my left.''

"I'll bet the CIA and the FBI and all of them are involved.''

"Without a doubt. But we can't be concerned about that

now. We have to find a away out of here tonight, if possible.''

"You think we'd be in danger if we just stayed through the whole thing?''

"I think we'd be pretty uncomfortable, no matter what happened. I don't think they'd be thinking too well of people who've been sitting around eating dinner with this dude.''

The shooting in the distance had come closer, nervous looks rippled around the table. Mr. Benjamin Lincoln, Mayor-elect of the city and one of the major rice blackmarketeers stood with a glass of scotch in hand. "I want to say welcome to Liberia, and I want to thank you for offering your support to my cause. Your presence gives my administration the good stamp of approval.'' He seemed to think that his remark was unusually funny and laughed for a long time.

"I know that some of you all are worried about that rabble on the outskirts of the city. I can assure you that they will be wiped out before I assume the office of mayor this Sunday.''

Chester and Valaida exchanged looks of disbelief. Was this guy joking, or what? "Valaida, we have to get to our embassy to get out of here. We'll just take a couple bags and all the money we got.''

"I'm ready when you are.''

"Let's ease out when they reach the mingling after dinner stage.''

The mingling after dinner stage took place two hours later, after a sumptuous dinner that was enlivened by fierce automatic rifle fire and a dance troupe from the interior. Valaida's Liberian dinner companion leaned over to whisper, "These little buggers were here when my forefather's came to this country.'' The drinks were strong and as the evening moved on, the conversations and behavior became more erratic.

"Now's the time," Chester whispered into Valaida's ear. They eased away form the gathering, smiling and bowing graciously, the thud of mortars zeroing in on the establishment. They quick stepped to their apartment.

"Valaida, no, don't take all those clothes, honey! We can get some more clothes!" They made a surreptitious exit from a side entrance and wound up on the dark side of the State House. Chauffeurs lounged around their highly shined limos, gossiping. Chester made an impulsive decision. "Uhh, pardon me, my friend, I wonder if I could persuade you to drive us to the American Embassy..."

"Oh, suh, I'm bery sorry, suh. I am the driver for Mr. Cornfog."

"Of course you are. I'll give you fifty dollars to drive us to the Embassy. You'll be back before Mr. Cornfog misses you."

"Fifty dollars, suh?"

"That's right. Fifty Americano dollars."

Epilogue 4

They were halfway to Accra, Ghana before they were able to pick up a newspaper, explaining what had happened in Liberia.

Opposing forces swept through the city, wiping out Benjamin Lincoln's defenders. A bomb dropped on State House during the third day of the revolt killed twenty and wounded several others. The situation is now unstable and all visitors are advised to observe caution.

"Looks like they almost caught us back there, didn't it?"

"It was a lucky break for us, that we were able to get that last flight out." The American Embassy had been reluctant to help them out of the jam, at first.

"Well, Mr. and Mrs. Simmons, as you can see, things are a bit chaotic here and we have to be careful of whom we're dealing with. We could only assume that you all are close friends of Mr. Lincoln's."

"Look man, I told you twice already, we were invited to

this man's inauguration, we had no idea what was happening. Shit! We still don't know what's happening. What we want is out!''

Accra gave them example of what could be expected when the worst and the best wrestle with each other. The telephone system was the pits but W.E.B. Du Bois was buried there. The people were proud of their independence, but it was difficult to find toilet paper. They decided to skip upcountry to Kumasi. From a wild revolution to the drums of Kumasi was a giant move.

"You've still got those Kutero drums in your head, huh? The ones you heard in Casamance.''

"Yeah, you got that right. Those sounds are pretty hard to forget.''

The drum festival in Kumasi was magical. They danced with groups of thousands, all enjoying the same rhythms, being healed, excited, African.

"Are you glad we came to Africa?'' Valaida looked around the sparsely furnished room, at the bed that never seemed to offer them the same lump in one place at the same time, at the friendly lizard they had nicknamed Rufus. She swayed over to Chester, in her kente cloth negligee, half high on palm wine and the humidity.

"Chester Simmons, I am having the absolute time of my life. I am so glad that we came to Africa. I don't know what to say to you.''

"Even though we ran away and left a few of your favorite dresses in Liberia?''

"My mother always told me, don't go through any changes about stuff you can replace.''

Kumasi was Pamplona, the Cannes Jazz Festival, an old-fashioned-Revial in-the-tent, New Orleans Jazz Festival, the Watts Towers Arts Center, Day of Drum. Heavy stuff. They followed the ceremonial parade of royal drums into a soccer stadium and felt the vibrations that pulled some of them into religious ecstasy. They felt the healing powers of the drums.

"I never knew how important the drum is 'til now."

"Don't feel bad, baby, same thing here.

Kumasi, a young priest, so full of knowledge and light that his charcoal-tinted skin glowed, gave them a reading. "You will come back to Africa to live."

They were tripped out by the idea, intrigued. "That was a helluva thing for that young dude to say."

"And it sounds so true that I believe it."

"Sorta grabs you, doesn't it?"

"Really!"

Chester will always remember another priest, a woman strolling up the side of a hill with two trussed up chickens.

The guide had warned them about taking pictures of the beautiful old woman with the cowries bandoleer across her chest. "Suh, this lady does not like you to point the camera at her." Later, after the film was developed, he discovered the ten frames he had used to surreptitiously photograph here were blank.

"Valaida, check this out, baby. Ain't no way these frames should be blank."

"Kwame told you she didn't like to have her photo taken."

They both got sick for a few days in Lago, Nigeria.

"Chester, how do you feel?"

"Lousy."

"What hurts the most?"

"My heart, I think."

They felt frustrated, delighted to be in the most populated country on the continent, shaken by the poverty and corruption. Everything was greased with a little 'dash'. If you wanted a decent table in a good restaurant, the maitre d' had to be 'dashed'. If you wanted to do the most ordinary thing, someone had to be 'dashed'.

"Chester, weren't you the one who told me that Nigeria had cleaned up its act?"

"Guess I was wrong."

They look a long, crowded, slow bus trip up to the north, to Kaduna. "May be, if we get out of the big city we'll see another kind of country." They were fascinated by the throb and color of the crowds, the millions of activities that took place wherever they looked. Valaida didn't like Kaduna. "This Muslin thing is a bit too chauvinist for me."

"Yeah, I feel that way, too."

The orthodox Muslims of Kaduna felt relieved when the Simmons headed back south. They were sick of the African-American couple who seemed so unwilling to follow the exact letter of their social order.

Back in Lagos they were invited to have lunch at the American Embassy.

"How do you feel about going?"

"Well, to be frank with you, I'd feel much better if we hadn't received this invitation." They both nursed memories of Liberia and the last meal they had shared in an official residence. The American Ambassador, a medium sized brown skinned graduate of Notre Dame, was starved for football news.

"We can see games by satellite but its not the same thing, you know? If you're really a football fan you really have to be there, to live through it, to freeze in the stands."

They left Nigeria with a number of mixed emotions.

"What happened to all the oil money?"

"Who benefited from the oil money?"

"How can the government allow its people to live like that?"

"It's almost like some place else we know. The rich get richer and the poor get poorer."

The African world went from complete chaos to absolute

order in flashes. Chester and Valaida laid back to take it all in, rejecting and accepting as they saw fit. "I think the slave trade impoverished the west coast in a way that people can't imagine. It might be centuries before those forests can grow again. It's amazing that we still exist."

The simplest piece of business might be complicated by a piece of paper that no one could find. But it was balanced off by the level heads of the people, who sang and danced at odd times of the day or night, who smiled and moved along, no matter what.

A short stopover in Angola. The country had been devastated by the wars that they had suffered through. "Just think, it all stems from the Portuguese colonization. They left the country wrecked in every possible way, but history will ignore that. What they do is focus on all the problems that the African had trying to reconstruct their country."

"That's the nature of racist thinking, sweetheart."

Next stop, Azania.

They boned up on Azania as though they were preparing for a major league college degree. Nelson Mandela's successor was keeping the promises that the ANC made. The Afrikaners were now simply members of a subtribe, they had no more or less power than their numbers warranted. Small guerrilla bands of Afrikaners, those who freak out after independence and the Change was voted in, roamed the outskirts of Pretoria, but they were considered more nuisance than threat. They were mostly men in their fifties, embittered by the Change. They received no aid or comfort from the people and the American right wing had finally given up on them. They were down to almost eighty members.

The country worked. It was one of the most efficiently run countries in the world. Scandinavian efficiency experts sent their brightest people over to study the Azanian techniques. The Azanians had survived slavery in the 20th century, fighting for their right to be free people, stone by stone, person by person, family by family, group by group. The 'slaves' freed themselves, battling in a way that most people in the world had never known. When the Change was put into effect many Afrikaners committed suicide. They felt they had nowhere to go. The African people, the Azanians, blossomed like gorgeous butterflies. The years of suppression were pushed back with gigantic explosions of art, music, song, dance, drama, living.

Some visitors said it had the feeling of pre-AIDS Brazil, with a purpose. Chester and Valaida strolled the boulevards of Johannesburg, feeling spaced. They subconsciously stared into the faces of the African people, especially the ones who had survived the Holocaust. "Look at the old man's face, Chester, Have you ever seen so much pain in anybody's face?"

"He's old enough to have gone through that period when they were simply labor units and not allowed to see their families."

A number of Afrikaners, mostly industrial barons, were put on trial for crimes against humanity, after independence was won. The African people surprised the world by its evenhanded treatment of their former oppressors. There were no bloody scenes. No wholesale massacres, no revenge. The Afrikaners who decided to stay in the country were given the same opportunity as all the rest of the people.

Chester and Valaida looked down onto the broad avenues of Johannesburg from the twenty-third floor of the Sisulu Building. They were feeling solemn.

"Baby, you know something? I love this country, but I find it hard to laugh and make jokes up in here."

"I can get into that feeling a bit. What is it that bothers you the most?"

Chester stared at the couple across the room. A white

203

couple. "I think it's the memory of what this place was like, remember the television shows we saw, where they were whipping babies and burying people?"

"I'll never forget it."

"That's what gets to me. I sometimes have the feeling that I'm walking through a place that was a concentration camp for Africans." Valaida stared into the distance, chilled by the image his words set up in her mind."

"Yeah, I know exactly what you mean."

They spent two weeks in Azania, tripping from the north to the south, from east to west.

"Chester, I think it's time to go back home."

The return home almost put them on a lecture circuit. Everyone wanted to hear about their trip to Africa. They pushed themselves away from the circuit after a month. "Hey, we better get out of this before it's too late." Two months later, spending a Sunday with the *New York Times* and the *Augusta Herald*, sprawled out in their bed they suddenly looked at each other as though prompted by a common thought.

"When do you want to leave?"

"Well, since it's going to be for a long time we ought to take our time and really square things away here. How about next month?"

They made reservations for Dakar the following month, ignoring the people who tried to discourage them.

"What're you guys going to do over there?"

"A helluva lot more than we could ever do over here."

They both looked forward to the small village in Senegal and the sound of the Kutero drums.

Personal Sketches
of Los Angeles

SECRET MUSIC

BY ODIE HAWKINS

Utilizing the same thrust, power, and formula that made his *Ghetto Sketches* his first bestseller, Odie Hawkins moves the focus from Chicago, where he grew up, to Los Angeles, where he has lived for the past twenty years. And, once again, he has peopled his story with unforgettable characters; there is the telephone freak who drastically changes the lives of several of his victims, bringing ruin to a young virgin, death to a housewife, and happiness to a lonely old woman. Here is a mixed bag of odd lots that only Hawkins could invent. Or does he invent them?

TO KILL A BLACK MAN

By Louis E. Lomax

A compelling dual biography of the two men who changed America's way of thinking—Malcolm X and Martin Luther King, Jr.

Louis E. Lomax was a close friend to both Malcolm X and Dr. Martin Luther King, Jr. In this dual biography, he includes much that Malcolm X did not tell in his auto-biography and dissects Malcolm's famous letters. Lomax writes with the sympathy and understanding of a friend but he is also quick to point out the shortcomings of both Dr. King and Malcolm X—and what he believed was the reasons for their failure to achieve their goals and to obtain the full support of all their people. And he does not hesitate in pointing a finger at those he believes to be responsible for the deaths of his friends. "A valuable addition to the available information on the murders of Martin Luther King, Jr. and Malcolm X," says the *Litterair Passport*. Louis Lomax gained national prominence with such books as *The Black Revolt, When The Word Is Given*, and *To Kill A Black Man*. At the time of his death in an automobile accident he was a professor at Hofstra University.

SCARS AND MEMORIES: THE STORY OF A LIFE

By Odie Hawkins

Scars and Memories is Odie Hawkins' deeply personal story of his life's journey, from a childhood in Chicago where he was one of the "poorest of the poor" to highly paid Hollywood screenwriter with his own office—and those people, mostly women, who mattered to him along the way. *Scars and Memories* is a tough, gritty book about a survivor who, as a child, lived in dank, cold tenement basements where the cockroaches were so thick on the walls he could set fire to them with rolled up newpapers, where there was seldom enough food, where sex and drugs were as commonplace as summer rain and winter chill. This is a deeply personal story, sometimes painfully told, that only a writer of Hawkins maturity and skill could write. Odie Hawkins is the author of the novels *Chicago Hustle, Chili, The Busting Out Of An Orindary Man, Ghetto Sketches* and *Sweet Peter Deeder*